Hello!

Wow! I've had the most incredible day! Well, I'd just arrived at the studios to film my latest video which — guess what? — they're putting on the Bliss channel playlist! My security guy Jude helped me out of the limo, and I started signing autographs for the fans who were waiting to greet me. As I got down the line, smiling as they snapped pix and sent them to their mates, I saw the most gorgeous boy standing in the crowd...

Yeah, right!

That's what I wish my life was like. But I suppose I should stop daydreaming and write about my real one. This is meant to be a diary, after all. Well, okay, in real life I'm Hannah, and I live in St. Albans with my mum and dad.

My dad's called Sam and Mum's Charlotte. She only works part-time at the town hall doing admin-type stuff, so she's always here when I get home. Dad instals computer systems and he's usually back by half six – in time for tea. Afterwards, he sometimes helps me with my homework or does a couple of hours' paperwork in his study and then he and Mum sit down and watch the news and maybe something else and then go to bed. Not exactly thrilling, huh? You can see why I'd rather write about a made-up glamorous life!

Actually, something a bit exciting did happen yesterday. Dad had to go to Paris for work – how cool! Not that Mum seemed to think so. I don't know why she's in such a bad mood about it. Anyway, I hope he brings me something nice when he gets back tonight!

It's Saturday today, which means helping Mum do the supermarket shop and then going riding. That would be fab if I didn't spend half the time thinking about how much fun Maya and Beth are having without me. They're my best mates, BTW. Me and Maya used to ride every weekend, but now she goes round the shops in town with Beth instead. They go to New Look and try stuff on, and to Boots to test out make-up and all the different Impulse body

4

sprays. They did ask me to go with them a couple of times, well, Maya did, and of course I'd *love* to do all that stuff, but I've always said no because of riding. I'm jumping whole courses now and I'd really miss Pumpkin, the cute chestnut mare I usually ride, if I didn't see her every week. Well, I pretend that's the only reason I don't go, but what I hope they never find out is that Dad wouldn't let me anyway. I did ask a few weeks ago, but he just said no, not without adult supervision, as he calls it. Can you imagine? Us three all hanging out and doing stuff like putting the tester eye shimmers on each other with Dad standing there! How embarrassing!

Beth was on about buying the *High School Musical 3* DVD today, but I've made them absolutely promise not to watch it without me if they end up going back to hers.

It's down to Maya and Beth that I'm writing this at all, actually. I got this lovely purple notebook yesterday, when us three popped into the shop over the road after school. Beth said she was getting a pink one to make into a diary, to write down all her top-secret gossip, blushes and crushes etc., and Maya said she was getting the yellow one, for her poems and stories. I said I didn't want one, because I couldn't think what I'd do with it. "Write about your life, Han," Beth giggled. "Well, I mean, you'll have to get one first!"

I know she was only saying it as a joke and I did manage to smile, but it made my insides go a bit squidgy, like when you eat too many doughnuts, and I couldn't think of anything funny to say back. So I still wasn't going to buy one, but then she got really giggly and loud in the shop, so Maya did too (typical!), and the assistants were looking at us in an annoyed way. They have a note on the door that says only two schoolchildren at a time, which Beth says is discrimination and illegal, but still, I picked up this purple notebook. That way we could just pay and get out of the shop before we got thrown out.

"See you, Hannah!" cried Beth as she and Maya linked arms. Maya turned and gave me a little wave as they walked off.

"See ya!" I called, forcing myself to sound bright and cheery while a pang of jealousy shot through me. You can go round one way or the other to Maya's. She used to walk via my house until Beth persuaded her that it was quicker and easier to go

6

her way, which is in the total opposite direction for me. So I've ended up walking home on my own the past few weeks and I hate it. It makes me feel like Maya's chosen Beth over me, which she hasn't, it's not like that. Well, maybe it is, kind of. Oh, I don't know! All I know is, me and Maya have been friends for so long, just us two, since the start of juniors, I guess I never imagined anyone else joining on. We're a three with Beth now and I try to act as happy about it as those two are, but secretly I'm not – not really.

I don't want to sound mean to Beth or anything, about her being loud in the shop (and everywhere else!), because she's really nice. But it's just that so much has changed since she came, and it's making me feel kind of left out. Like, me and Maya used to be the same level of loud as each other, and now that Beth's joined in with us and she's more loud, Maya's become more loud too. At first I tried to be louder as well, but I just sounded all weird and fake.

And, well, they do this thing where one of them suddenly starts a song and the other one joins in. I want to as well, but I feel too embarrassed about my rubbish voice. And sometimes they get into complete hysterics in PE or something, and I'm kind of half joining in but half feeling a bit silly, like I'm just pretending. And it seems like me and Maya don't do any of *our* stuff any more, like passing notes in our secret-code writing or making up silly rhymes where we do a line each. Beth got too impatient when I tried to teach her our code and I did start a rhyme off a couple of times with the three of us, but she just got annoyed when she couldn't think of anything and said it was babyish, so now Maya won't join in either.

The other thing is, we don't hang out round here (I mean, my house) after school now we're a three. It used to be fine with just me and Maya, but when I asked Beth over too it didn't go that well – i.e. she said loudly how she found it weird that we had to take our shoes off in the hall, and sit down at the kitchen table with Mum and Dad to have tea, and do the drying up and putting away afterwards. And when Mum came up to my room when we were making up a dance routine and asked us to turn the music down, Beth gave me such a look – I nearly DIED. When Mum left the room, she said, "Well, what *are* we going to do, then?" in this stroppy way, like there was nothing else interesting in my entire house. We ended up playing Monopoly. I tried to act really excited and get them into it, and Maya didn't seem to mind, but I could tell Beth found it really boring.

So now we go to hers instead. Her mum doesn't get in till six so we can do what we want. And we help ourselves to stuff for tea from the freezer, put it in the microwave then eat in front of the telly. It's not as much fun as it sounds, though, cos Beth usually suggests games for two people, like tennis on the Wii, and my go never quite seems to come round, so I have to sit there reading mags by myself and pretending I don't mind, or fiddling about with my phone, acting like I'm too busy texting to even care what they're doing. I'm not that into going round there, to be honest, but I'm worried that if I stop, those two will get even closer.

You're probably thinking, Well, why not just find someone else to hang round with? but it's not that easy cos everyone in my class has been in their same groups since we started high school and you can't just break in. And anyway, me and Maya have been BFF since Year 4 and she's the nicest person I've ever met and I'm not going off with someone else for anything. I wasn't going to write this, but my secret, secret worst fear ever is that they might go off without me, and I can't stand to even think about losing Maya.

Tuesday

Can you believe, it turns out those two watched *High School Musical 3* without me?! At break I was chatting on about how I couldn't wait to see it when we're next round Beth's, and they both looked really guilty. Beth said, "Well, the thing is, we watched it on Saturday, when we got in from the shops. We just couldn't wait, and it was so good."

I just stared at her, and I got that sicky, squidgy feeling in my stomach again. It was meant to be a thing for all of us to do together. We were going to line up the armchairs in a row and have microwave popcorn and Cokes, to make it like being at the cinema.

"Beth really couldn't wait to see it," said Maya quickly.

Huh! I thought she would have been like, No way, we promised we'd watch it with Hannah so we are going to wait, but she wasn't. I couldn't hide how hurt I felt. She nudged my arm and said, "You don't mind, do you, Han?" Well, I did mind, but what could I say? Then she turned to Beth. "She could take it home, couldn't she?"

Beth shrugged. "Yeah, sure."

I wanted to say, *That's not the point*, but I didn't. I just tried to look cheerful instead.

I've decided that I'm going to keep on writing in here, because it's quite nice, letting my true feelings out, just totally in private. It's as if having them on the page stops them from going round and round in my head. So it makes me feel better about annoying things like *High School Musical 3* (a bit, anyway). I'll have to find a good hiding place for it, though, just in case anyone decides to have a snoop round my room!

Tuesday still, after tea

Something weird is going on round here. I was just coming out of the bath and Dad's mobile went and instead of pacing up and down the hallway talking on it like he usually does, he said, "One moment, please." Then he dashed up the stairs into his study, gave me a don't-be-nosy look and shut the door behind him. I was going to try listening in, but I couldn't really because he'd seen me there so I'd probably get caught, plus I was pretty cold in just my towel.

I wonder what he doesn't want me to hear?

Or maybe it's something he doesn't want Mum to hear (she was in the kitchen pottering around, so in ear-range of the hall too). I don't think it could be secret from her, though, because they tell each other everything, even stuff they shouldn't (like when I really begged Mum not to tell Dad about us buying my first bras and she did anyway and then he mentioned it at dinner and I nearly DIED of embarrassment).

Anyway, I just heard him go downstairs now, so I'm off to ask him what's going on.

One hour and 22 mins later

Huh! When I asked what was up, Dad just said,

"None of your business," and Mum said, "Nothing," both at the same time. Well, it can't be nothing and none of my business, can it? It has to be something in the first place to be none of my business. Huh! If they're going to treat me like a little kid and not include me, then I'll just have to work out what's going on for myself.

A little bit later

I was just reading my *Girlsworld* mag and I got to the problem page and saw this thing about friends. It wasn't exactly the same situation as me, Maya and Beth, but it was pretty similar, and it made me decide something. I'm just going to tell Maya how I feel. She's so lovely, I'm sure she hasn't been meaning to make me feel left out. Claire from the mag says you and your BFF should be able to share your secret feelings and support each other. By not saying anything, I haven't really given Maya the chance to do that. I'm sure she'll make more effort to include me if I just say how I've been feeling, then Beth will have to as well.

Wednesday, after school
That didn't go very well

Beth had to stay behind after Maths and go over something she'd got confused on, so I found myself going out for break with Maya. She doesn't do her loud thing when it's just us two, and we were walking round the playground having this really good chat so I decided to say something. I took a deep breath and went for it. "You know, I miss it being just you and me."

Maya looked at me, a bit surprised. "Me too, sometimes," she said, "but isn't Beth great? She was so funny in assembly today, I thought I was going to burst out laughing!"

"Yeah," I said, secretly thinking how I'd seen Mrs. Andrews watching us, and mainly been worried about getting told off in front of the entire year.

"And her house!" Maya went on. "It's amazing. Isn't it fab having somewhere to hang out with no adults on our case?"

"Yeah," I said again. "I just, sometimes it's a bit…"

Maya turned and looked at me. "Han, is this about that DVD?" she asked.

I blinked at her. "What?"

"I told you, Beth was really desperate to see it, like, *really*."

"It's not that…well, not just that. But it's, well, you always walk home her way, and go round singing together, and spend Saturdays with her in town."

Maya just looked at me blankly. "But it's quicker for me to go via Beth's. And *you're* the one who won't join in singing with us and can't make Saturdays." She flicked her hair, seeming impatient, annoyed even. I knew she didn't like me talking about Beth that way.

I felt really flustered. When Maya put it like that, each thing on its own did sound like nothing. "I know but… It just feels like she's taking you away," I finished lamely, feeling like a total five year old.

Maya sighed. "Course she's not, Han. Me and you will always be bezzie mates, just with Beth now, too. Don't worry, she really likes you."

"That's not what—" I began, but then trailed off.

I changed the subject after that. There was no point trying to explain. She just wasn't *getting* it.

SOOOOOO FRUSTRATING!

It feels like we can't *really* talk to each other any more. So much for that problem-page advice! Now I feel even more on the outside. Even worse, Maya is going round Beth's tonight without me, cos I've got to go to the dentist. OMG, I've just thought – I hope she doesn't tell her what I said. She wouldn't, would she? What if I've just made things ten times worse for myself?

ARGH!

I hate this situation, and I still don't know what to do about it.

Thursday still, in bed

Me and Mum watched *High School Musical 3* tonight (Beth finally remembered to bring it in – and she's being alright-ish with me, so maybe Maya didn't say anything – phew!). I didn't tell Mum about those two watching it without me, because I don't want her getting in a huffy mood with Beth – if she thinks they're leaving me out she might not let me go round there any more. And if I don't, I'll have, like, NO chance of seeing Maya outside of school.

Dad was meant to be watching it with us, but we had to wait ages for him to stop fiddling about in his study. He kept saying, "Five more minutes," which always means at least fifteen. After AGES he finally came down, but then his mobile rang and he went upstairs to answer it (with the door shut again).

We paused the DVD, and I said I'd go and hurry him up, but Mum didn't want me to and eventually we started it again without him. When he came back down again, he said he'd give it a miss because it wasn't his thing anyway, and he had lots of paperwork to sort out upstairs.

I was a bit disappointed, but I wasn't *that* bothered. That's why it surprised me when Mum gave me a strained smile and said, "Just a minute, darling," in a fake cheerful way, then followed him out into the hallway. I hit pause, so I could hear what she said. You need to listen quite hard when my parents are having a row because they don't shout, they just do this hissy-whispering thing. It was something like, "Sam, we've been hanging around waiting for you half the evening. It's not about whether this film's *your* thing; it's about being interested in your daughter's things."

I thought Dad would come back, because he usually does what Mum wants if she gets upset, but he just said he really did have a lot to do and then I heard his footsteps on the stairs. "Hannah matters *too*!" Mum shouted then. I didn't get what she meant, and I don't know why she made such a fuss – it really wasn't a big deal. Actually it was quite good because after that she went and got the box of posh chocs Dad had brought back from Paris for her, and said we should tuck into them without him, seeing as he was being such a grump.

Then we settled down to watch the rest of the film and it was good, but not as good as it would have been with Maya and Beth. I mean, it's not Mum's fault or anything, but I could tell she wasn't really that into it, even though she was acting interested. It's much better sharing that kind of stuff with mates. I have to find a way to skip riding on Saturday and go into town with them. I don't want them to keep spending time without me, or they might go off altogether. If I just tell Mum and Dad how important it is to me, hopefully they'll understand and say I can go after all.

Friday

It was awful at school today. When we were walking around at break, Beth and Maya started this song I hadn't even heard before and it made me really panic for some reason. Even though I hadn't had a chance to talk to Mum and Dad about it by then, I found myself blurting out, "I'll meet up with you guys in town tomorrow. I need to find some nail polish to go with my new blue top and—" But the way they were looking at each other stopped me dead. "What?" I asked.

Maya stared at her shoes as she spoke. "Well, it's just, Beth's mum's got invites to the opening of this new beauty spa—"

I folded my arms and glared at her. "Yes?"

She glanced at Beth pleadingly, but Beth didn't step in, so she stumbled on. "Well, we're getting all these free treatments and—"

"I can come to that then," I said. I felt so awkward, inviting myself – why hadn't they asked me in the first place? Why hadn't they even *told* me about it?

"Ooooh, I'd love you to, Han, but not poss," said Beth breezily. "It's very exclusive – tickets are like gold dust, Mum says. We were lucky to even get four, and that's Mum, her friend Susie, me and Maya. Sorry." She didn't sound it. I felt sick.

Once again I forced on my fake smile. "Oh, it's fine. I should probably go riding anyway," I said, trying to sound breezy too.

"That's what we thought," said Maya awkwardly, "that you were already busy, so you couldn't come anyway. And we didn't say anything about it in case you felt left out."

"Yeah, exactly," said Beth, like she'd only just thought of that.

"Sure, no worries, have fun," I said, and then I managed to change the subject.

Help! I have *got* to do something about this before I lose Maya completely.

Things are really weird at home, too. Dad's gone away for the night, to Paris again. I didn't think anything of it, because it's just a boring work thing (I was actually a bit pleased because last time he brought me back an Eiffel Tower key ring and mug). But then something happened that made me think he's not telling me the whole story.

When Mum said where he'd gone, I put on a funny French accent and started going, "*Ooh la la, Maman! Papa* is in Par-ee again! But *pourquoi* would he have to go there for his boring old work? Perhaps *mon père* is in fact not a computer manager but an international spy or secret undercover journalist, *non*?"

I was only messing around, but the look on Mum's face stopped me in my tracks. She was so upset, and I have no idea why. I asked what was wrong but she insisted she was fine, even though she was stood there in front of me, like, nearly crying. Now I'm thinking that maybe these Paris trips have got something to do with the shut-door phone calls. What on earth is going on?

Saturday

Even though we did loads of jumping (my fave) today in my riding lesson, I could hardly concentrate, thinking of Maya and Beth at that spa without me, chatting and laughing and (probably) telling each other secret stuff like who they fancy, and listening to each other's problems.

Dad got back from Paris at about four o'clock and of course I asked straight away what he'd got me. But he just looked really stressed and said he hadn't had a chance to go in any shops. And then about an hour later, he and Mum were arguing, like properly shouting at each other and I don't think it was because she didn't get any chocolates this time.

When I went downstairs they stopped and the atmosphere was so awful I didn't dare ask what the row was about. They were supposed to be going out with some friends tonight, but Mum phoned them

24

and said she had a headache and now she's gone to bed early. And Dad's shut in his study again. At least it means I don't have to go round to our neighbour Mrs. Millett's (they would never let me stay in the house on my own, even though I've been twelve for ages now). But I don't like it that they aren't getting on. It's horrible sitting here by myself just, like, worrying about them. In fact, I think I'd rather go next door and spend the night in front of the telly trying to explain to Mrs Millett which one is Ant and which is Dec.

Sunday

After lunch, me and Mum went to look round the Open Studios, where you go into artists' houses and see where they create their paintings. Dad said he'd stay at home because he had a few calls to make for work, and instead of saying, Absolutely no way, it's Sunday, Mum just said "fine" in a voice like it wasn't fine at all. It's so strange – even when he's really busy, Dad *never* works on a Sunday. It's one of their things, that we have to spend the day together as a family.

Anyway, we went to a pottery studio hidden at the bottom of the artist's garden and then we visited a painter's house that was all higgledy piggledy with brightly-coloured walls and strange objects everywhere and when we came out again we both agreed that the house was actually more interesting than the art!

The last one we saw was just this white room

which this girl who only looked about eighteen had filled with her beautiful paintings and sculptures of ballet dancers. It was brilliant and it made me wish I had some artistic talent (which I don't!). Mum did enjoy herself when she got into looking at things, but it was obvious that she was mainly only being cheerful for my benefit. Even the carrot cake and tea we had in the Corner Café afterwards didn't put a smile on her face. Part of me wanted to ask what was wrong, but I didn't because I was frightened of what she might say. That's because I've started to get this nagging thought about what might be going on between her and Dad. Quite a scary thought, actually.

Oh. That's weird. I just tried, but I can't make myself write the words down in here. It's as if writing it might make it come true or something. I'm sure it's not that anyway. I'm probably just going on my usual Hannah worrying thing that I can't seem to help doing, even if nothing's really wrong. Honestly, I'm terrible like that. Even when I just lost one of my trainers before PE, I was having a full-scale panic by the time I found it under the benches five minutes later. Anyway, I'm sure the scary thought's not true. It can't be. Can it?

Monday lunchtime

I'm in the library because I want to be by myself. I don't feel like hanging around outside with Maya and Beth. Not after what happened at first break today.

Well, it was…

The thing is…

I ended up crying.

I never cry, but I couldn't help it. One minute I was getting an apple out of my bag in the cloakrooms and the next I was a sobbing mess on the floor and Maya had her arm round me. I didn't want anyone to see, so we hurried over to our hang-out place on the furthest bench from the netball courts. Beth tripped along beside us, looking more excited than concerned.

Last night the scary thought went round and round in my head until I finally fell asleep, but it was still there this morning, getting stronger and bigger and whirling like a tornado until there was no room for anything else in my head. I felt like I was going to explode if I didn't talk about it.

Maya sat next to me on the bench, still with her arm round me. Beth plonked down on my other side and said, "What's up, Han? Don't you feel well?"

"I think my parents are splitting up," I gabbled, letting the scary thought out at last. Then I started crying again.

"Hannah, you don't really think that, do you?" gasped Maya. "There's no way it can be true."

"Oh no! You poor thing!" Beth cried. "If you're not going to eat that apple, can I have it?"

Sighing, I handed it to her and she took a big bite, spraying juice all down my jacket.

Maya squeezed my hand. "What on earth's given you that idea?"

I sniffled and gulped, trying to keep my voice steady. "It's, I don't know – they just don't seem to like each other very much any more. They've started arguing, and Dad's been going to Paris for work and staying away overnight. He's never done that before

— I think it's because he wants to get away from Mum."

"That or he's having an affair," said Beth, through a mouthful of my apple.

I guess it's lucky I wasn't eating it myself, or I would have choked. An affair? I hadn't even thought of that.

"Of course he's not," Maya snapped, her arm tightening around my shoulders. "I'm sure it is just a work thing, Han. And don't worry about them arguing, everyone's parents do, it's normal. My mum and dad argue all the time and they're still together. They even had this really big rough patch when Radha was playing up, going out every night, but they sorted it out. People don't split up just like that. They try and make it work first."

I felt so much better when she said that. Until...

"My parents didn't," said Beth. "Mum told Dad to get out the night she found out about Ffion. Everything was perfectly fine up until then. Things were great, in fact, because he felt so guilty. Like, he was always buying me stuff and bringing Mum flowers."

I thought of the chocolates from Paris and felt sick.

Maya gave Beth a sharp look and she fell silent, apart from the apple-crunching. But she didn't have to say anything else – I already knew the story. Her dad had moved out into a hotel that same night. Then he rented a flat with Ffion who, it turned out, he'd been seeing for nearly a year before Beth's mum found out. Then Beth's house had to be sold as part of the divorce and they moved to a much smaller one on the new estate at the edge of town. Then Beth had to change from private to state school and that's how she ended up starting at Meakin High, just after Christmas. Beth really hates Ffion and she'll do anything to get out of visiting her dad. She's supposed to go every other weekend but she's always got some excuse ready. When I asked her once if he minded that, she said no because he's not bothered about seeing her anyway. And she's got this idea that now her mum's single, she'll meet a rich film star and remarry and they'll move to Hollywood and have a fabulous life and that will show her dad who's won. Like, as if.

Whenever she's talked about her family set-up before, I've thought it sounded dramatic and interesting – you know, like living in a Jacqueline

Wilson book. But now when I think I might be in the same situation, well, it just seems like a terrifying nightmare I'll never wake up from.

Anyway, I must have looked completely devastated because once again Maya started insisting everything would be fine.

"Yeah, maybe," said Beth. "Anyway, check out my pedicure from Saturday." She started pulling off her shoe and sock. "I so wanted to wear my peep-toe boots in today to show these off. Mum said it was fine, but you know what Mrs. Davis is like – the old bag would have had me in detention."

"Beth!" Maya gasped. "How can you talk about your toenails at a time like this?" She pulled me even closer to her and, as Beth glanced at me, I saw something flash in her eyes. Jealousy. Unbelievable! Even at a time like this, she was annoyed about my own best friend giving me attention!

"Maya, there's nothing more to say about Hannah's parents," she said haughtily, then she turned to me and added, "I told you, they're all the same, men. Your dad's an idiot for having an affair."

"He's not having—" I began, but Beth was unstoppable. "He'll only get dumped in the end and then he'll be all alone and he'll be sorry and wish he'd never gone off in the first place. That's what Mum says."

Maya gave her another sharp look, but she ignored it and I was too busy trying to catch my breath to tell her to shut up. "It'll be good for your mum in the long run," she added blithely. "She could do so much better than him anyway, if she got some new clothes and had her hair done."

Honestly, she might as well have punched me in the stomach.

"Beth!" Maya shrieked, but she was on a roll, full of enthusiasm. "Hey, maybe we could all take her shopping and—" She gabbled on and on, but I didn't hear any more. The bell went for the end of lunch and we started walking back into school.

Beth had gone off ahead to check her hair in the loos, but luckily Maya was still holding on to me, because I stumbled and nearly fell. It was horrible – I suddenly felt like I couldn't walk, like I'd forgotten how. I looked right at her, clinging tight to her arm. "They're not splitting up, are they?" I whispered.

"No, of course not," she said, but she wouldn't look at me. I knew Beth had got her wondering.

I think she was as freaked out as I was, because we didn't say another word about it.

So now my head's spinning like a fairground ride. Instead of making me feel better, telling them my fears has just led to even more questions, and even more doubts. Who's Dad talking to, shut in his study upstairs where Mum can't hear? Is Beth right about an affair? If she is, does Mum know what's going on?

I feel like I'm standing on the edge of a cliff, with the ground crumbling away under my feet and nothing to hold on to.

Monday still, but the evening

I cannot BELIEVE what just happened. Okay. Deep breath. I need to start from the beginning and get everything in order in my head. Not that any of it seems *real*, but –

Right, well, it all started when I walked into the house tonight. Weirdly, I could hear Dad's voice coming from the kitchen. He usually doesn't get in until 6.15-ish and it wasn't even 4. I heard Mum too and I was about to burst in as usual, but then a stranger's voice, a woman, made me stop at the door. She spoke too softly for me to hear, but Mum's reply was loud enough. "Yes, of course we'll discuss it with Hannah," she said, sounding impatient, "but we need to be sure we're definitely going down this route first. We don't want to unsettle her unnecessarily."

My heart started hammering in my throat and I was thinking, *Unsettle me about what?* Even though I tried to stop it, my brain started thinking that they were talking about the dreaded D word.

"Hannah, is that you?" Mum called, so then I had to go in.

The woman had frizzy red hair, cut in a kind of wedge shape, and green-framed glasses. She was closing these files in front of her. She didn't look like a solicitor. But then, I thought, maybe they don't wear suits all the time. Or maybe she was a marriage counsellor or therapist or something. She slid the files into a big patchwork bag, then looked up and smiled at me and went, "Hi Hannah, I'm Julia." I hated the way she said it, like she knew all about me, when I had no idea who she was, or why she was there.

"Erm, hi?" I mumbled.

She stood up. "I'm just off now."

As Dad got up to show her out I didn't say *Goodbye,* or *Nice to meet you.* My head was getting fuzzier and buzzier as Mum got me some juice. When Dad came back in, I suddenly found myself blurting it out, the dreaded words flying across the room like missiles. "You're splitting up, aren't you?"

There was silence.

"Aren't you?" I yelled.

Then I felt Mum pulling me into a fierce hug. "Oh, Hannah," she sighed. I felt so angry I pushed her away. Then so scared I fell back into her arms.

Dad was looking at me like I was speaking Japanese. "Hannah, where on earth did you get that idea from?"

"The phone calls, the trips," I yelled, then my voice cracked with tears. "And Beth reckons—" I trailed off. I couldn't be bothered to tell them what Beth reckoned. I felt so tired and confused.

"Oh dear God," Mum muttered.

"I didn't realize..." Dad said. "I can't believe you thought..."

Mum gave him a terrible look, like this was all his fault, and said, "Tell her, Sam."

Dad looked ashen. "I'm not sure how to say this, but... Perhaps I should just come straight out with it." He breathed out slowly. Then he said, "Er, well, the fact is that you have a 15-year-old sister."

"Half-sister," Mum snapped.

I just stared at him. "So you're not getting a divorce?" I asked, my voice catching in my throat. "There's no other woman in Paris?"

"Hannah!" Mum cried.

"No," said Dad. "Eloise, Ellie...she lives in Paris. I've been going over there to see her – and to sort things out with the authorities. That's why I've been on the phone a lot too."

I blinked at him. "So you're really not getting divorced?"

"Hannah, for the last time, I promise you we are not," Mum insisted. She looked as pale and shaken as I felt.

Finally, I took it in. I've heard people say they were flooded with relief, but I've never felt it before, not like that. It felt really real, like someone was pouring warm honey right through me. Every muscle seemed to relax and my mind stopped swirling around by the ceiling and came back into my head. Everything wasn't ruined – our life as a family wasn't over.

"Hannah? Han?" Mum had been talking but I hadn't heard a word. "You do understand what your dad's saying, don't you?"

That was when I stopped thinking about them splitting up and started to absorb Dad's words. "I've got a sister?" I repeated. But it just wouldn't go into my head. It was like him saying I had three arms or something. "I've got a sister," I said again, but it still didn't seem real.

"*Tell* her," Mum ordered.

I remember thinking, *Tell me what? There's more? But how can there be more than this?*

"Ellie's mother is in hospital," Dad said gravely. "They were in a car accident. Ellie got off fairly lightly, but Celeste is in a bad way. So she can't look after Ellie at the moment."

I was going to ask what exactly had happened, but I was so stunned I forgot to. There was only one thing going round in my head by then, one thought booming out.

I'VE GOT A SISTER.

"Why didn't you tell me about her before?" I asked.

Dad sighed. "I only found out three weeks ago, when I got a call from the hospital staff in Paris. It's as much of a shock to me as it is to you."

"And to me," said Mum, more to herself than to us.

"Yes, well, it's a surprise to all of us," said Dad briskly, "but Ellie needs our help." He paused. He actually looked nervous. Of *me*. "The plan is for her to come and stay with us."

I have a sister. Coming *here*. I could hardly take it in.

"How long for?" I asked.

"We're not sure," said Dad. "At least a few weeks, maybe a couple of months."

"Well, we'll have to see about that," said Mum. "We've agreed to take it one day at a time for the moment."

"But we *have* made a firm commitment to social services to care for her while Celeste is unable to," Dad said, to me, but kind of to Mum as well. "This girl is my daughter – she's family."

It sounded so weird, him saying "daughter" but

not meaning me. I felt Mum's hand on mine and when I looked up, she said, "You're our first priority, Hannah. And if you're not okay with her coming here, it won't happen." She looked straight at me, as if Dad wasn't even there.

"She wouldn't have to share my room, would she?" I asked. It's weird what you say when you're in shock.

"Well…" Dad began.

"Of course not, darling," said Mum, giving him another one of the killer looks. It suddenly dawned on me that this was why they'd been arguing so much. Mum doesn't seem exactly keen on the idea of Ellie coming to stay. Or the idea of Ellie *at all*.

"Okay, no, you won't have to share, not if you don't want to," Dad said then. "I'll move my computer things into the dining room and Ellie can have my study."

"Sam! She hasn't even agreed to it yet!" Mum snapped.

They both looked anxiously at me. It's hard trying to think with people staring at you. I mean, I knew I wanted to meet Ellie, and it seemed like the right thing to do, you know, to help her out while her mum was in hospital. I couldn't really see why not. "I guess it's fine," I said uncertainly.

Dad smiled, but Mum didn't. She said, "Hannah, we're not asking you to make a snap decision. You need to have a proper think about this. It will be a big adjustment for you and—"

But Dad cut in. "If she says it's fine, it's fine."

I thought Mum would say something back, but instead she just pursed her lips.

"When can she come?" I asked.

"Friday, all being well," Dad replied, avoiding Mum's glare.

Wow. So soon. Like, this week.

That's when it all seemed too much to take in, and I just had to get away. "Can I go upstairs?" I asked.

"But, Hannah, don't you want to discuss—" Mum began, but I just grabbed my juice and the biscuit tin and headed up here. I needed some space cos I feel like my brain's been bent round and tied in a knot. I also wanted to write down what had happened. And now it's here on the page in actual words, it's starting to seem more real.

I still can't believe it, though. This is the most

incredible thing that's ever happened to me in my entire life. And there I was expecting the worst. I really thought my mum and dad might split up, but instead I've got a sister! Well, half a sister. A half-sister, I mean. A teenage one, too. From Paris.

I feel so nervous and so excited and so scared about meeting Ellie.

OMG, what if she doesn't like me? Or what if I don't like her, and I've just agreed to her staying here? Maybe Mum was right and I should have thought about it more, but I was so shocked at the time I could hardly think at all, and if I go back on it now, Dad will be really disappointed. And anyway, I'm sure she'll be fab and loads of fun. But what if—

Oh, my brain is whizzing round so fast my pen can hardly keep up!

What if she thinks I'm too young to hang around with? But maybe she'll like having someone younger to look after. A younger sister! OMG, I'm someone's younger sister! That sounds so weird! I wonder what she's into? Maybe she rides, and we can go together. That would be brilliant. Or even if she doesn't yet, she might want to give it a try. I could help her, like lead her round for the first couple of lessons, and show her how to tack up and check her stirrups. But I guess, even if she's not into that, we can do other things together, like going to the ice rink and bowling and the cinema.

Oh, hang on, I can hear Dad coming up the stairs. I'll go and grill him about Ellie. I was so shocked before that I forgot to ask any questions, and she's coming this week, and I don't know anything about her.

Tuesday after school

I woke up this morning and it wasn't a dream – there really is an Ellie and she really is coming to stay. On Friday. As in, in three days' time.

Last night when Dad came up, we made a start on moving his stuff out of Ellie's room (Ellie's room – how mad is that?!). While we were untangling and ravelling up about twenty million computer cables, he told me loads more about her, like how she's coming to my school for as long as she's here and how the language won't be a problem (which I was wondering about), because she's bilingual (French and English). Turns out her mum, Celeste, is half English and they've travelled all over the world and haven't only lived in France. I wanted to ask Dad loads of things about Celeste too, like how they met, and where, and if they went out for long, and if he was in love with her. But when I tried my voice got stuck in my throat. I think it was because I sort of wanted to know about him and Celeste and I sort of didn't – like my brain was curious, but my heart wasn't so sure. So instead I made him tell me all about Ellie.

She sounded more cool and glamorous with everything he said (like how she's into art and music and fashion) and I started getting butterflies in my stomach. "I can't wait to meet her," I told him, "but I'm a bit nervous. I mean, I hope I like her."

"Oh, you will. She's lovely. Very pretty, and so sparky," he replied, puffing up with pride, and being dense as usual (i.e. not getting what I really meant, which was that I hope she likes me).

I told Maya and Beth the whole Ellie story at school first thing this morning (I nearly texted them last night but I decided to wait so I could see the looks on their faces!). It was great because Maya was so excited and pleased for me. But Beth was a bit sulky about it, especially when it got round the class at registration and Jecca and Nadia came up. She always tries to impress them and now they were interested in me instead. They wanted to know all the juicy details, like if Dad had had an affair behind

45

Mum's back, or if he'd kept Ellie secret from us for years, or if Ellie was really rich and might buy me an iPhone and loads of cool stuff from Jane Norman. I had to say none of that was true, but the real story still had them hanging on my every word and going, "No way, Han!" and "Cool, Han!" and "Oh. My. Gosh, Han!" I loved the way they called me Han, not Hannah, like we're mates, when normally they hardly even notice I exist!

It was also great at break time, because me, Maya and Beth hung round on the benches with me in the middle, not Beth, for a change. Maya was talking about the cool stuff her sisters sometimes do with her that me and Ellie can do together as well. Beth's an only child so she just had to listen (which made her even more moody, but that's not *my* fault!). As she went quieter and quieter it felt like me and Maya were just a two again.

Maya reminded me about this time when Radha, her eldest sister, who's 16, took her to this Indie gig in this tiny basement under a bar. Maya was dancing round with all Radha's teenage mates and they kept buying her Cokes and crisps because they thought she was really cute. It wasn't even secret or anything

– her mum was fine with it because she knew Maya would be okay with her big sister. I know Mum and Dad wouldn't let me go to something like that even if I was with Ellie, but I didn't say so. Instead I acted like of course they would and even grumpy Beth had to look a bit impressed. I felt really cool and it did make me think that now the evenings are getting lighter maybe me and Ellie can walk into town together, like Maya does with Radha and Sharmin. We could go and hang round at the skatepark and watch the boys and buy smoothies from the cafe stand and sit at one of the tables outside it and talk about...well, everything! I'm sure Mum and Dad would let me do that.

I've been thinking of a few more things we can do together too, which are:

1. I can sneak into Ellie's room at night and we can tell each other secrets and talk about private stuff.
2. We can go to the cinema and watch films and share a big bucket of popcorn (I hope Ellie likes the sweet kind, same as me).
3. She'll probably be a fab cook, from living in

47

France, so we can do baking together. We could make a big chocolate fudge cake, then eat it while we're watching a DVD. I hope we like the same stuff, but of course I won't mind watching what Ellie likes.

I didn't go round to Beth's tonight – she said she felt sick and hurried off as soon as the bell went. Probably sulking about how much me and Maya were chatting together today. I didn't care though, cos it meant that Maya didn't go either, and she walked round MY way home instead – YAY!

So after today I'm feeling a bit more excited than nervous about Ellie coming. Like, maybe about 40% nervous and 60% excited.

Oh, that's Dad back. Gotta go down and set the table for tea. Bye!

Tuesday night

Oh, typical – I've been in bed ages and I still can't sleep so I opened my eyes again and now it's 12.23. I think I'll go and get some juice.

Tuesday night still, no, hang on, Wednesday morning

When I went downstairs just now I found Dad still up, sitting at the kitchen table with the little lamp on. "I can't sleep," I said.

He smiled. "You're not the only one. Come here."

Even though I'm too old (what would Beth think?) I sat on his lap and he showed me the pictures he'd been looking at. They'd come out of a tatty shoebox and smelled kind of fusty. They were from a really, really long time ago, like before I was even born. There were lots of Dad with these people I didn't recognize, doing stuff like messing around in a park and on a riverbank, then at a party, all grinning into the camera with their arms round each other.

"How come I don't know any of these people?" I asked.

Dad frowned. "I suppose I've lost touch with my old friends over the years," he said. "Once you start a family you get so busy it's easy to let things slide. Besides, your mother wouldn't let most of them into the house. She always thought they were a bunch of chancers, the Motley Theatre Group."

"You were in a *theatre group!*" I cried. "Doing what, opening and closing the curtains?"

"Shush!" hissed Dad, pointing at the ceiling. "The cheek! For your information, young lady, I was one of the actors and I got some fairly major roles, so I couldn't have been *that* bad, could I?" He shuffled through the photos then pulled one out. The various people in it were all standing together, grinning at the camera with their arms round each other. "There we all are," he said with a smile. "The Motley Crew."

I scanned the faces and found Dad. "Nice haircut!" I sniggered. "And as for those trousers – call the fashion police!"

"Ha ha," he went.

"What kind of plays did you do?" I asked then.

"Oh, anti-capitalist, anti-Thatcherite, socialist-themed stuff. Usually written by our Nev there." He pointed out a grinning, wiry-haired man. "It's not like I had a burning ambition to be a systems installation manager, you know. I wanted to be a professional actor. It was such a great feeling, being up there in front of an audience, telling a story, being someone else. It was magic."

Dad's eyes glinted in the lamplight as he spoke and I saw something in his face I've never seen before. He was almost kind of sparkling, like I was when I first cleared a double on Pumpkin in my jumping lesson and everyone clapped us.

"We used to stay up all night talking politics; we were going to change the world," he said.

It's weird how I've never thought about Dad's life before he had me, or what he was like when he was younger. I've always just assumed he's been the same ever since he grew up, apart from having less hair now and a bit of a belly.

Dad shuffled on to the next picture. "Oh," he said.

He tried to hurry on, but I put my hand on his – I wanted to look at it properly. I knew it was Celeste from his reaction.

She was really beautiful, with striking blue eyes and long dark hair. She was smiling up at the camera from where she sat on a swirly rug, wearing a kind of shirt-dress thing, dangly earrings and a scarf in her hair. Either side of her, other people's knees and elbows had made it into the picture, and the air was hazy with smoke.

I wasn't sure I wanted to know about him and Celeste but he started telling me stuff anyway, while staring at the table. "Hannah, I'll be honest, I was in love with her," he mumbled. I desperately wanted to shove my fingers in my ears and go, "La la la," but I made myself nod and look at the picture again, to show how mature I am. "We spent a few months together, that's all, though it felt like longer. Then she went off to India with hardly a word. At the time I was heartbroken, but I knew deep down that no one could keep her in one place. She'd never settle down; she was a free spirit."

It just came out, before I could stop myself. "Do you still wish you were with her?"

"Oh, Han, of course not! If we'd stayed together, I'd never have met your mum and had you." He squeezed my arm. "And you two are the most wonderful, precious people in my life."

I felt better then, but also **very** embarrassed because Dad doesn't normally say things like that.

"You know, I think she left because she found out she was having Ellie," he said then. "I mean, all this time and I didn't know. I hadn't left the area, she just had to call directory enquiries. One call. I mean, it was easy enough for Ellie to contact me last month…" I could tell he was angry with Celeste for not telling him she was pregnant, for not giving him the chance to be involved. Then he sighed. "Oh well, what's done is done."

"I should be getting back to bed," I said. I felt like being on my own, to think about things.

"Sure," he said. "Oh, but, Han, you should know – Celeste's consultant rang. It looks like she's going to be in hospital for longer than we thought – it could be a few months. Ellie's pretty upset about it, on top of everything else. When she gets here, please don't keep asking her about the accident. Let her tell you about things in her own time, when she's ready."

"I won't mention it," I promised him. I can only imagine how Ellie must be feeling. There was a six-car pile-up on Casualty last week, with crushed legs and punctured lungs and firemen cutting the car roofs off with giant chainsaws to get people out. It looked so terrible that the only way I could keep watching was to remind myself it wasn't real life.

But it actually did happen to Ellie, and now her mum's seriously ill in hospital. Of course she won't want to talk about it. She's probably still in shock.

"And I'd appreciate it if you could stay off the subject of Ellie going home," Dad said. "I'm not trying to keep her apart from Celeste or anything, it's just that there's no point upsetting her when she really can't go back yet. I want her to have a proper chance to settle in here first. If she insists on going back now, to be near Celeste while she's in hospital, she'll only end up in foster care, or a children's home, and kids can really go off the rails in those places. We can offer her something better than that – some stability and emotional support. So I need you to help take Ellie's mind off it all, okay?"

"Dad, it's fine, I understand," I insisted. "Whatever you think will help Ellie the most is fine with me. I want her to like being here."

He tucked Celeste's picture in near the back of the pile and wrapped his arms round me, saying, "Thanks, Han, you're a sweetheart."

We looked at one last photo, of him with some of the guys from the theatre group all wearing giant Mexican hats and silly fake moustaches. "And

you're an idiot, if that photo's anything to go by,"
I told him.

"Charming!" he hissed, poking me in the ribs.
"Anyway, off to bed now."

So I'm back up here, but I still can't sleep!

Wednesday night,
writing this in bed

We went round to Beth's after school today and did our hair. Her mum's got loads of straighteners and curling tongs and styling stuff, and Beth loves experimenting with it all. It was fine when we were looking at mags on her bed to get inspiration, cos we were all chatting together, but then when we got started the usual thing happened.

Beth was absolutely **desperate** to go first, so Maya put her dark brown curls up in an actress-on-the-red-carpet style she'd torn out of Grazia. Then Beth actually **washed** Maya's hair and deep conditioned it. When she'd dried it off a bit she did it all poker-straight with the tongs and shine spray, which took **ages**. I tried to get involved, passing them brushes and holding the towels and things, but I felt like a spare part. Then, by the time it was my turn, Beth was *desperate* to eat (she always seems *desperate* about something) so we ended up going downstairs to get our dinner. They promised I'd have my turn afterwards, but in the end there wasn't time. I don't know if Beth planned to miss me out or not – but after me and Maya chatted so much again at school today, she was even *more* all over her and even *more* off with me than usual. At least having pizza was good – it was a proper shop-bought one, with microchips, and I didn't have to have any salad with it like at home.

I've just thought, I really *will* have to keep this diary secret now! Beth must never read this, or even Maya, and not Mum, of course, or *anyone* in fact. Not with the things I've just written!

We carried on sorting out Ellie's room when I got back (Sita, Maya's mum, dropped me home), and now it's all ready for her, which makes the whole thing seem even more real. We've put the chest of drawers from the conservatory in (we emptied out the DVDs, and most of them are going to the charity shop, cos they're far too babyish for me now anyway). Mum borrowed a bed from her friend Rachel and we made it up with my purple duvet set and put Jasper my rabbit on top to greet her. I really hope Ellie likes her room and our house and, well, everything!

Thursday
I don't want to go to school tomorrow!

I really want to go with Dad to collect Ellie on the Eurostar instead, but Mum said, "No way". She won't let me miss school for anything, not even something as vitally important as meeting my sister! It's one of her things, not missing school. Even if my leg was hanging half off or something, she'd probably just put a bandage on it and wheel me up there in Dad's office chair. Oh well, hopefully the time will go quickly, and I'll hurry straight home as soon as the bell goes.

I can't believe Ellie's coming tomorrow! My stomach does this weird lurching thing when I think about it, like it's trying to jump out of my body. I'm back to 70% nervous and only 30% excited now. And I'm still thinking stuff like What if she doesn't like me? and What if Mum's too strict with her? (V. v. cringeworthy!)

I wonder if we'll like the same food or find the same things funny on TV? Dad didn't know, and he doesn't have a picture of her either. And when I asked if she was really fashiony or more Emo, he didn't even understand what I meant! ARGH! Useless! I suppose I'll just have to wait and see for myself.

Friday, she's here!

When I got in Mum said Ellie was upstairs unpacking and before she could get another word out I raced up there straight away, but then my nerves kicked in and I hovered around at the top of the stairs, my heart pounding. I'd been planning to go in and do that two-cheek-kisses thing, but in the end I felt too shy so I just poked my head round the doorway and went, "Hey," and she went, "Hey," back. Then I wondered if I should introduce myself but that felt kind of stupid seeing as she already knew who I was.

Poor Jasper was squashed under her suitcase with just one eye and a folded ear sticking out. She must have put it down on top of him without noticing. I really wanted to rescue him but I managed to stay put, cos that wouldn't look too cool, and anyway, I was far too busy staring at Ellie.

Okay, I'll describe her in detail, so you get why I was going WOW.

Well, she is really, really, not just pretty but actually beautiful and she has amazing hair, which is long and shiny and really dark brown with cool red streaks in. It sort of falls round her face in this lovely way with no stupid curly-up sticky-out bits like I get. She's got big blue eyes which looked even bigger and bluer because of all the dark blue eyeliner and black mascara she had on, and she was wearing this really short, fairy-ish floaty dress with tights, and these separate stripy sleevy things that came down over her hands. It looks really fab, but there's no way Mum would let me wear an outfit like that cos she'd say it wasn't a dress, but a top. She'd make me wear jeans with it, which would completely spoil the effect. Hey, I've just thought – maybe now that she's seen how nice it looks on Ellie, Mum will start letting me wear stuff like that too!

Ellie didn't talk to me or anything, she just gave me a smile and went back to her unpacking. I wanted to say something but my mouth was so dry and my brain was so blank with nerves that no words would come out at first. Then, once I did start talking, I couldn't stop. I was going on about how we cleared the DVDs out of the chest of drawers for her, and how I liked her dress and shoes and butterfly hairclip, and how cool the clothes were that she was taking out of her suitcase. Suddenly I realized I was going on and on and on and not giving her a chance to say anything, so I made myself shut up.

Ellie looked straight at me with her brilliant blue eyes (I wish my eyes were like that, instead of boring brown). "I'll need a mirror," she said. She had only the softest touch of an accent and it wasn't the same as totally French people sound when they're speaking English. I hadn't heard anything like it before. Maybe it was unique to Ellie, after growing up in lots of different places.

Then my mouth was off again, going, "Sure, I'll ask Dad, we could put one there on the wall, or maybe you'd like one on that chest of drawers, to make a sort of dressing table. Do you need it right now, cos you can borrow my one if you want or—"

Just when I was making myself look like the uncoolest, most boringly-rambling-on girl in the entire universe, Mum appeared in the doorway and I managed to zip it. She smiled at Ellie, but it was like the smiles I do when Beth's telling a story more to Maya than to me and I'm just standing there listening. A kind of strained smile. "Dinner'll be ready at 6.30," she told Ellie. "I didn't know what you like so I'm doing fish fingers and chips. That always goes down well with Hannah. I hope you're hungry."

Ellie smiled shyly at Mum. "I suppose," she said softly, still gazing at her suitcase. "Do you think it would be all right to have a shower and change first?"

"Of course," said Mum. "I'll get you some towels."

"Thanks." Ellie took her cool spangly purple washbag from her suitcase and followed Mum into the bathroom. Before I realized it I'd followed them both in too and Mum was saying, "Come on, Hannah, give Ellie some space." I felt like an idiot again so I came in here to write this. On the way I nipped back into Ellie's room and grabbed Jasper from underneath her suitcase. I felt sorry for him, being squashed like that, and I'm glad Ellie didn't see him after all – I bet she'd think he was massively babyish!

Ellie's still in the bathroom. MY SISTER is right there, in that bathroom! SHE IS AMAZING!!!

I know she hasn't said much yet, but it's not like I gave her the chance, is it?! I really wish Mum hadn't told her I liked fish fingers. I mean, how babyish does that sound? Tomorrow I'll have to get her to cook us Beef Bourginone (however you spell it!) or something wrapped in Parma ham. Then I can say that's my new fave.

Oh, I have to go now – time to set the table. Ellie will probably talk more at teatime, and I can fill her in about school and stuff. I could tell her about Mr. Thornhill doing that cringeworthy guitar-playing in assembly while wearing sandals with socks. That really made me, Maya and Beth laugh. Hopefully Ellie will find it funny too.

I'm writing this in bed – I can't sleep cos my mind keeps going over everything that's happened!

When Ellie came down for tea she was wearing another cool dress, light blue this time with sequinny bits. It was still as short, and she was still wearing just tights with it (purple ones now). I loudly said how nice it was, hoping Mum might start getting the hint to let me wear things like that too.

We all sat down and at first it was a bit awkward with no one saying anything apart from, "Please pass the ketchup" and, "Would you like some orange?" When I filled up Ellie's glass with squash she gave it this *look*. She didn't say anything but I bet she was thinking she was way too old for it. From now on, I'm having plain water, or even better, I'll ask Mum if we can have those posh fizzy drinks in glass bottles like cranberry and elderflower.

Just like me, Dad couldn't stop staring at Ellie. Mum couldn't either, but she had this strange smile fixed onto her face, like she gets when people come round and don't take their shoes off at the door. Luckily Ellie looked mainly at her plate, because otherwise she would have just seen these three people eyeballing her and probably thought, *Oh help, they are so weird, what on earth did I come here for?*

Mum took charge after a while and asked her a few questions and soon we were talking almost normally. I really wanted to ask Ellie about the car crash and how painful the faded cuts and bruises on her arms had been, and what it was like going in an ambulance, but I didn't of course.

Then Dad asked her if she liked her room and when she said yes, almost as much as her room in Paris, he looked really pleased. She said she wished she'd brought the curtains over with her, that her mum made from Indian saris, to finish it off.

It's cool how Ellie sometimes calls her mum Celeste, it sounds so sophisticated. I wish I could call Mum Charlotte but I know she'd go nuts.

Anyway, Ellie said that Celeste paints and writes poems as well as making things out of fabrics. Mum was nodding politely and Dad was still staring at Ellie with a dazed look on his face, like he couldn't believe she was actually real. I was going, "Wow, that's amazing, she sounds so creative and talented. You never do anything like that, do you, Mum?"

Mum said, "Well, I'd like to but I don't have time, I'm too busy looking after you," and Dad did a loud clearing his throat thing.

Then there was a bit more silence and so Dad started acting extra-jolly and told a story about this funny thing that happened in the office yesterday, except that it wasn't very funny as it turned out. But even though Mum and Ellie didn't laugh, I did, because I didn't want him to feel bad.

Then I told Ellie my Mr. Thornhill story (I wanted her to realize that at least one of us knows what humour is) and after that she told me about this music festival she went to with her mum when they were living in Spain in a camper van. I was really pleased that I'd been the one to get her chatting. The festival sounded amazing – they lived in a community with other people in vans and trucks and stuff (and this one family even had an old bus) and they just hung around in the sunshine playing guitars and dancing and doing yoga. And she's lived in India and Thailand too. How amazing! And the music festival she was talking about was held in this dried-up riverbed, and it lasted three whole days, and it was massive with thousands of people. They saw all these great bands and Ellie was only seven but she could just go round on her own and make new friends.

"I wish it was more like that round here," I said, then added, "I wasn't even allowed down the shop on my own till I was eleven!"

ARGH! Why did I bring that up? Between that and the fish fingers, Ellie must think I'm a total baby!

Thank goodness she just carried on talking like she hadn't even heard. When she finished, Mum said, "That sounds fun, but wasn't it difficult to keep up with your education?"

Ellie just shrugged and speared her last few chips with her fork. "We didn't really worry about that too much," she said. "I did go to school in some places, if we stayed for long enough, but Mum taught me at home mostly. School turns everyone into unthinking zombie cut-outs, brainwashed to slot into an impoverished western culture and maintain the status quo."

Well, that made Mum do her eyebrow-raising thing.

"Life experience is much more important, that's what Celeste always says," Ellie went on. "But I have been going to school in Paris for the last couple of years, on and off, and it was okay. I did like being in the handball team."

"I'm sure you'll get on the netball team at Meakin High too," boomed Dad, still doing his jolly voice, "and they have lots of other groovy activities."

Yes, in case you're wondering, I did nearly die of embarrassment when he said "groovy". No one

Dad's age should be allowed to use that word. But Ellie didn't seem to notice, luckily. Instead she just shrugged and said, "I suppose."

Later, as I cleared the table, I was rambling on about getting some games out or watching a film when Ellie asked if we minded her just listening to her iPod in her room for a while and then having an early night. Mum and Dad both said, "Of course not," and I tried to hide how disappointed I felt.

Usually when I go up to bed I get a kiss and a hug from Dad, then Mum comes to tuck me in, but they didn't know what to do with Ellie. Mum smiled at her and started wiping the table and Dad gave her a kind of half hug thing that turned into a back-pat. I just said, "Goodnight, or *bon nuit*, as they say in Paris," and did a stupid giggle. Duh! What is WRONG with me?! Could I have made myself look any *less* cool in front of Ellie? (Answer: NO!)

When she'd gone upstairs, Dad said, "Never mind, love. You girls will have plenty of time to do things together. Ellie's tired from the journey, and she's been through a lot recently. Just be patient, okay?"

"Okay," I said, but I still felt like a balloon when half the air has leaked out of it – kind of saggy and limp. I'd really been hoping we could hang out together tonight, so that I could somehow reverse the rubbish first impression I've made.

Anyway, I'm going to try getting to sleep again now.

It's Saturday!
My first proper day with Ellie!

I'm about to go downstairs and watch some telly now. Maybe Ellie will come down as well when she wakes up. I might put one of my *Hannah Montana* DVDs on. I wonder if they have that in France? It'll be cool if she likes it already, but also cool if she's never seen it cos we could watch all the episodes together from the beginning.

And maybe she'll come along and see me ride later! I forgot to ask if she likes horses or not – she might even want to book a lesson herself for next week if she does.

Saturday still

Me and Ellie are having such a great time! We've just stopped for lunch – can you believe we've been doing up my room?! I'm sitting here on a sheet on the floor, surrounded by paint pots and brushes! I wasn't expecting to redecorate, but what happened was, Ellie knocked on my door at about ten this morning after I'd come back upstairs to get dressed. She came in with her hair dripping from the shower and went, "Can I borrow a wide-toothed comb...oh."

I didn't know why she went "oh" at first so I said, "What is it?"

She wouldn't tell me for ages and I had to really coax it out of her. Eventually she sighed and said, "It's just not what I was expecting. I mean, well, erm, maybe the pony posters are a little..."

"What? Babyish?" I demanded, feeling a bit annoyed.

"A bit," said Ellie. "And that cream paint is just..."

"Boring?" I snapped.

She grimaced, and nodded.

"Oh. Right," I said stroppily. I was a bit put out because I'm not used to people walking in and criticizing my stuff. Apart from Beth, obviously.

"Oh, Hannah, please don't be upset," Ellie

begged. "It just came out wrong. I didn't mean it in a *bad* way."

"Huh!" I huffed, pouting.

"I just meant that because you're a really cool girl I thought your room would be too. Not that it isn't—"

I softened and gave her a small smile. She was tripping over herself to make up with me by then. And she *had* just said I was cool, after all.

Suddenly I was looking round my room and it was like I was seeing things through new eyes and realizing how rubbish and worn out and boring it looked. "You're right," I admitted. "The walls were that colour when we moved in here, and as for the pony posters, they've been there since I was *eight*. Maybe it's time for a change."

I stood on my bed, reached up and started to carefully peel back one corner of the nearest pony poster, of a grey Welsh pony, lifting the Blu-tac with my thumb first so that it didn't pull the paint off the wall. Then I felt like I didn't just want my room to be different, but I wanted my*self* to be different too – more like Ellie and more grown up and more fun and just *more*, somehow. Before I knew it I'd ripped the poster in half and snatched the rest from the wall.

Ellie was astonished.

So was I.

Then she burst out laughing.

And I did too.

She leaped onto the bed and reached for a bay Arab mare at the top of the wall. She pulled down hard and there was a lovely loud tearing sound and we both burst into giggles again. Then we were jumping all round the room pulling down the posters, whooping and giggling with these silly grins on our faces. As Ellie passed my stereo she flicked on the radio and turned up the volume to about 3,000 decibels so there was music all around us. When we'd finished tearing off the posters we danced round and round with the bits of torn paper, whirling and twirling.

Then suddenly, Dad burst in. "What's going on in here?" he demanded.

I absolutely froze. I thought he'd go mad when he saw the mess. I tried to catch Ellie's eye, but she was staring at the floor.

Amazingly, though, Dad just smiled and said,

"I'm glad you two are having fun. And if you're, ahem, redoing your room, we may as well do it properly. I'll take you to that DIY place and we can choose some new paint, seeing as you've pulled half that old stuff off with the Blu-tac anyway."

"Really? What, today?" I asked. "But don't you have stuff to do?" Dad usually has to work for at least half of Saturday.

He shrugged. "Nothing that can't wait."

For a moment it felt unfair that he's suddenly being all cool and nice because of Ellie, when he's normally really strict with just me. But I only minded for a second. Then I realized that I don't really care why the change has happened. I'm just glad it has.

"Thanks, Dad, that would be amazing," I said.

"Yeah, thanks, Sam," said Ellie.

Then Dad said, "Oh, and if you could just turn the stereo down a bit that would be groovy. It's not me, I don't mind, but Charlotte doesn't like it too loud."

Ellie looked up and we both smiled at him and nodded and then when he shut the door we burst into fits of giggles again and collapsed on the bed. Ellie totally got that I was laughing about him saying "groovy", and it was so great that she found it funny too, with neither of us having to say anything. Maybe we're more alike than I thought! If only I had her looks and hair too!

So Dad took us to the DIY store at the retail park and we chose this lovely light blue paint for my room, almost the same colour as Ellie's dress, and we got a big canvas of bright pink flowers to go right over my bed. Ellie said she's going to get me some mags so we can cut stuff out like fashion shoots and pop-star pix and stick them on the wall, and when Dad heard that he bought me a giant cork board so I could pin them to it instead (he said Mum probably wouldn't be keen on having Blu-tac on the walls again, not when they're going to be all lovely and new and fresh). So then he got Ellie a pinboard as well, so she can make her own fashion-shoot collage, and we chose her a full-length mirror, like she wanted. Oh, and we saw these gorgeous flamingo fairy lights by the tills, so he bought us each a set of those too. I've never seen Dad flash the cash so much. Usually it's hard enough getting him to cough up my measly amount of pocket money!

Gotta go – I'm off riding this afternoon. I did ask

Ellie if she fancied coming along but she said she'd rather stay here and keep going on my room. That's so nice of her, and maybe next week she'll come along to the stables with me. I've just realized, me and Ellie have been having so much fun, I've hardly even thought about what Maya and Beth are doing in town without me. Oh, but now I've written that, I *am* wondering! Typical! Maybe me and Ellie can have a girly chat about it all tonight. Perhaps she'll know what I should do.

Sunday after tea
Today we finished painting my room,
and Ellie helped me solve a big problem!

Well, Ellie hung out in her room again last night, so we didn't get to chat, but I ended up telling her about the whole Maya and Beth thing while we were painting, anyway. I said how I think Beth only hangs out with me because Maya does, and how I don't invite them round any more because I know Beth doesn't want to come. I explained that I wouldn't mind so much if we hung out at Maya's, but they always want to go to Beth's instead. And I told her how they leave me out when we're round there, even though I was ashamed to admit it.

Then I ended up telling her about my secret, secret worst fear, you know, about how Beth might take Maya away completely and I'll be left on my own at school with no one to hang around with.

Ellie was silent for a moment, then she said, "Are you sure you even **want** them as friends? Sounds like they're not being very good mates to you."

"I know it seems that way," I admitted. "And maybe Beth isn't, but me and Maya have been BFF for years. Beth's come along this term and Maya has got really into her — it's like she's been hypnotized or something. She's even stopped coming to riding so she can hang out in town with Beth every Saturday. I reckon if I can keep in with them she might snap out of it and want it to be just us two again. Or maybe Beth'll start including me properly and we can be a real three. But if I stop hanging round with them now, that's it. They'll go off and I'll lose Maya for good."

"Well, maybe you could have a week off riding now and then, and go with them," Ellie suggested.

"I've thought of that, and I'd like to, but Dad won't let me cos he says I'm too young to be in town on my own," I explained, feeling totally embarrassed about it.

"Don't worry about Sam," she said, as if it was that simple. She put down her paintbrush and headed to the door, saying, "Come on, let's ask him again now."

Of course, as I thought, Dad said, "I'm sorry to

sound like an old fogey, Hannah, but you're not going into town on your own – you're too young."

"But it's not on my own," I protested. "Maya and—"

But Dad cut me off. "You know what I mean. And anyway, we've had this conversation already. You know where me and your mum stand on this. Maybe in the summer, when you're thirteen, but not yet."

I was just about to give up when Ellie said, "How about if we invite the girls here first to see Hannah's new room, and then I can go into town with them all and bring Hannah back afterwards?"

I just stared at her. What a fab idea! No way will my friends realize that she *has* to be there or Dad wouldn't let me go. And if they come here first they can see my new room and hang out with Ellie and they might want to start coming round again, so we're not always at Beth's. We waited, both staring hopefully at him. I thought he'd say no, or at least that he'd have to talk to Mum about it. But guess what? He said yes!

Ellie grinned at me and I grinned back. Go sisters! She went back upstairs but I stayed in the kitchen, getting us some apple juice. Dad said, "I appreciate all the effort you're putting into making Ellie feel welcome, Han. I'm really proud of you."

"It's no effort," I said. "Having a big sister's great. She's way more fun than *you*, meanie."

Then he poked my arm, so I jabbed him back and it turned into a wrestly hugging thing. At that moment Mum walked in from the utility room with a pile of neatly folded ironing balanced all up her front. We tried to pull her in too, but she got annoyed and asked Dad if he was *trying* to make her drop the clean clothes on the kitchen floor.

Then I told her about next Saturday and she got annoyed because she pays for my riding lessons up front at the start of each term. "We're not made of money, you know!" she snapped, then added, "And thanks for asking my opinion, Sam!" before marching off upstairs.

I looked at Dad – I didn't get why she was so annoyed. It was only *one* lesson. He grimaced and said, "It's okay, Han, she's fine – well, she will be. She just needs a bit of time to get used to Ellie being here." He didn't sound that sure though. I don't get why Mum wouldn't *love* having Ellie around and be happy that us two want to do stuff together. Maybe seeing Ellie all the time reminds her that Dad used to be with someone else, and that annoys her. But then, hardly anyone marries the first person they meet, do they? And it's not Ellie's fault she exists!

I hope Mum cheers up soon because she's kind of taking the shine off things a bit, to be honest. Me and Ellie were having such a laugh at lunchtime and she totally spoiled it by being too serious. What happened was, Dad announced that Gran's been on the phone and she's planning a trip so she can meet Ellie in the next few weeks. To give you a clue what she's like, I call her Strict Granny (not in front of her – like I would dare!). Just the mention of her makes Mum flustered. Before Strict Granny comes Mum usually cleans like mad all over the house, even the hidden bits like on top of pictures and down the back of cupboards. But somehow Strict Granny always finds something to complain about.

I was just telling Ellie what she's like and we got into giggles, and then it turned into complete hysterics, and I even exaggerated how bad Strict Granny is, cos making Ellie laugh felt so good.

Dad said, "Come on, Hannah, that's your grandmother you're talking about." But he didn't really try to stop us. I think he was probably desperate to join in himself!

And then me and Ellie started making up this silly poem about Strict Granny being a battleaxe and we were each adding loads of funny bits and trying to come up with a rhyme for "scary". When we came up with "hairy" we just couldn't stop laughing. I hadn't noticed Mum getting annoyed but suddenly...

"Hannah!" she snapped. "That's enough. Don't be so rude."

I was really startled. I don't normally get told off at home, but that's because I never have anyone to mess around with. Anyway, Ellie doesn't even know if her other grandparents are still alive, because her mum left home when she was sixteen and never saw them again. I was only trying to make it funny so that she didn't think about not having them and start getting upset (well, not only for that reason, but...). So I was actually being sensitive.

Then I was just thinking, how come Mum told me off and not Ellie, that's not fair! But I didn't say so cos I didn't want Ellie to feel awkward. It's not her fault Mum's so uptight. Ellie looked at the table and at first I thought she was upset, and I felt my stomach churning round with upsetness too, but then I realized that she was smiling and biting her lip and trying really hard not to burst out laughing. That made me forget being upset and want to start laughing too, so I looked at my dinner, cos I knew if we caught each other's eye we would just *collapse*.

We managed to be remotely sensible through our apple pie and ice cream, and when Ellie asked if she could be excused, I asked as well, instead of helping clear the table like I usually do. We raced upstairs and threw ourselves on her bed in absolute fits, and yes, we did finish off the Strict Granny poem in the end, but in secret! It was so much fun having someone to make up silly rhymes with, like me and Maya used to.

I've got to go now. Ellie said she hasn't seen any of the *Hannah Montana* DVDs so I'm putting one on for us to watch in the living room. That'll be one more thing ticked off my list of cool girly stuff for us to do!

Monday morning

Ellie's coming to school today. Mum's going in to work late so she can drive her there cos they have a meeting with Mrs. Davis, the head, before she joins her class. I'm getting a lift with them, so I've got some extra time to write in here.

Ellie just came downstairs in this amazing outfit of yellow tights with little pumps and a sort of vintagy-looking black and pink dress and a little black cardigan with two holes in it where her thumbs poke through. It's amazing how much she fitted into that suitcase – lucky her stuff folds down really small! And she's wearing all her lovely bracelets on her right arm, on top of the cardigan. I knew Mum was dying to tell her to go and change the tights for jeans *at least* but instead she just said, "We must get you a uniform at the weekend."

Ellie said, "Thanks, but I'd better see if I like the

place first, no point wasting money."

Mum did a pretend laugh and said, "School is not optional in *this* house, dear."

When I get home tonight I'm going to make a surprise for Ellie to say well done on surviving her first day at a new school. Not that she sees it as surviving. When we were talking last night after our DVD-watching session, she said she's looking forward to making some new friends. I thought that was so amazing. I mean, if I had to start a new school in a new country in the middle of the year, I'd be terrified that no one was going to talk to me.

I asked Ellie if she was nervous, but she said no, not really, cos she isn't that bothered what people think of her and anyway, she and Celeste moved so often she's used to making new starts. I didn't ask *why* they moved so much, because of promising Dad I wouldn't go on about things to do with Celeste. It's really hard not to because I'm desperate to know exactly what happened in the crash, and what her injuries are, and about Ellie's life in Paris before all this happened.

The hospital rang last night, but I don't know what they were saying because Ellie spoke really fast in French, and even though I'm in the second top set for that I could only pick out a few words. When Ellie came off the phone she was a bit disappointed that she hadn't been able to speak to her mum in person, but only the doctor. Dad said he was sure Celeste would call the second she was well enough, and Ellie did cheer up a bit after that.

I'm hoping she'll decide to talk to me about it all at some point, and I didn't promise Dad I wouldn't listen, did I? But last night she just went to her room with her iPod, without saying anything about it to me. Poor thing, she must be missing her mum loads already. Hopefully, when we get to know each other better she'll naturally start talking to me about how she feels.

Oh, Mum and Ellie are ready to go now — so bye!

Monday still, I've just come out of the bath and I'm lying on my bed

Poor Ellie wasn't that happy when she came home from school this afternoon. It's not that she didn't make any friends (she hung out with these cool kids

88

called Cara and Jed who I've seen around school) but the lessons are much harder than she'd thought. She reckons she missed some stuff when she was travelling around, and I said maybe she did, but also it could just be the difference between the French and English systems. Perhaps she's been learning different stuff, I said, and sooner or later they'll do something she already knows about and then she'll be ahead. That cheered her up a bit, and so did the surprise chocolate cupcakes I'd made (I rushed home on my own cos she had to stay behind and register at the school library and the IT centre, so I had time to whip them up). They'd gone a bit wonky because I hadn't checked the oven tray was flat on the shelf, but she didn't mind.

As she ate her third one, washed down with a big cup of coffee (I'm SO going to start drinking coffee too), she started to smile again. "Well, at least I'm in the top set for French," she joked.

Then she said about having Maths homework to do that she just didn't get at all, and I suggested she ask Dad for help, cos he's really good with figures. But she said "no way", cos she doesn't want him to think she's thick. I told her Dad wouldn't because he's not like that. We did have a teacher once called Mr. Donovan who *was* like that and he used to roll his eyes or tut loudly when you got something wrong. But then one day he threw a whiteboard rubber at Clarissa Morgan's head and we had a supply lady after that. Dad's the total opposite of Mr. Donovan and really patient. But Ellie still said "no way", so I helped her instead. I didn't realize it, but actually I've got quite good at Maths because of Dad helping *me*. I kind of ended up actually doing most of it, but I didn't mind because Ellie said thank you loads and told me I was really brainy!

When we were nearly finished, Dad came home, with two copies of a picture he took of us while we were painting my room. He'd printed them out on his really good laser printer at work and he gave one to each of us. Ellie looks amazing in it, of course, and I actually look okay for a change, too. Ellie said she could see a little bit of a likeness between us around our cheeks and nose. I could see it a bit too, after staring at the picture for ages – how cool!

I went, "We'll have to buy frames for these."

But Ellie said, "Let's make some. That's what I always do. Where's your craft box?"

I told her I don't have one because I don't really make things. Then I felt a bit of an idiot cos when I said, "Where can I get one?" she just laughed.

"It's not something you can buy ready-made, Hannah," she explained. "You put it together yourself from odds and ends that people give you, like leftover bits of material and ribbon and things like that." When she saw me looking embarrassed she smiled and added, "I'll help you start yours off. Find an old shoebox and we can decorate it with wrapping paper. And I'll see what I can cadge from the art room."

That's so incredibly nice of her. Dad looked really pleased too and said, "There's a craft shop in East Street that sells art materials – you could pop in after school tomorrow." Then he gave Ellie twenty pounds for us to spend there! Twenty quid! That's more than he's ever given me! I wanted us three to stay at the kitchen table hanging round and chatting, but Mum came in and hustled us out, because she had to get the tea on before her aerobics and she was running late.

It's great having Ellie here. It's like she's working a kind of magic on me and Dad. I feel like a whole

91

new Hannah, who's much more cool and fun than usual, and Dad's like a whole new dad, who's mega-generous and smiley all the time. And Ellie's going to try and help me fix things with Maya and Beth too. She's like my own personal fairy godmother! Well, fairy godsister!

I wish she could cast a spell on Mum, though, to stop her being so serious and bustly and muttery all the time. After tea I overheard her say to Dad that twenty pounds is an excessive amount of money to give Ellie, especially after everything he'd spent at the weekend. He said it was no big deal and she said, "You can't buy her affection, you know." That made Dad really annoyed and he went, "For goodness' sakes Charlotte, why do you have to read so much into everything? That money is for both the girls. There's nothing wrong with me treating them to a few art materials!"

I got butterflies in my stomach when he said "the girls". Me and Ellie are "the girls". Dad's girls. Having a sister is as good as I imagined it would be – better, even. I can't believe I was so nervous and worried before Ellie arrived – having her here is the best thing that's happened to me in my whole entire life!

Tuesday
I'm just quickly writing this while Ellie gets changed

We're going to make our photo frames in a min — how fab! Me and Ellie walked to school together this morning and then we met at the gate afterwards. It was so great cos loads of the kids in my year were staring at me, obviously wondering why I was hanging around with a cool Year 10. Jecca and Nadia even said "see ya" to me which they never normally do, and so did their friend from 8W, Anna, the one who's having a party on Saturday. From our class, only those two and some of the boys have been asked so far (including Tom who, OMG, is **gorgeous** — not that he even knows I exist). There's a buzz all round Year 8 about it and it would be fab if I could get invited. Even better, if I could get Beth and Maya in too, they'd think I was so cool. No way would they go off without me after that.

I felt so proud to be standing at the gate with

Ellie, especially when Maya wanted to come to the craft shop to buy art stuff with us too (she couldn't, though, cos she had to get home for her piano lesson). BTW, Maya said she could come on Saturday – she's desperate to hang out with Ellie (she wanted to go up to her on the field a couple of break times, but Ellie's always been in a big crowd of Year 10s with Cara and Jed and I've been too shy to introduce them). Of course, the second Maya said she could come, Beth did too. I know she's keen on Ellie as well – even though she's trying to hide it – and besides, there's no way she's going to let me and Maya hang out without her.

It was really gorgeous in the craft shop – I've never had a proper look in there before. We bought pink and purple feathers and glass beads and these strings of spangly sequins and still had £6.50 left over. Dad's going to be SO impressed when he sees he's got change! Oh, gotta go! Ellie's ready to start.

In bed now

Something not too good has happened, to be honest.

I'm probably just overreacting, like Ellie said. OMG, though! It still makes me feel all kind of weird and uneasy and sick when I think about what happened. And even worse, about what could have happened. I'm just having to take a deep breath to calm down, even now!

There we were, happily making our picture frames at the kitchen table. We made the basic rectangles out of card and glued bits of old padded envelopes round them and then we covered them in this yellow material from an old top of mine that Mum let us cut up. Without Ellie, I would never have thought of padding the frame out and mine would just have been this coloured-in card one that looked tragic, like it was off Blue Peter or something. Then we added the feathers and sequins and glass beads, and even though mine was a lot more gluey than Ellie's, it was still really good.

"They look great, like they could have come from a shop," I said.

"They need a finishing touch, though," said Ellie, grinning. "I've got a surprise for you, Han. Look in your bag."

I blinked at her. "In my bag?"

She nodded, still grinning at me. "Take a look. Go on."

Well, I was really excited and thinking "How cool!" as I pulled my bag from the back of my chair and began rummaging inside. "Oh!" I gasped, as I saw the purple silk flowers and pulled them out. "Oh, I loved these in the shop!" I cried. "You got them for me!"

Ellie beamed. "Yeah, I saw how much you liked them. Cool, huh?"

"Yeah, wow, thanks!" I went. But that's when I started to feel uneasy. Something wasn't right. I'd seen the price of those flowers on the box. They were £3.50 each. We'd left them because we couldn't afford one each along with all the other stuff we'd bought. And I was sure I hadn't seen Ellie go up to the counter by herself to buy them afterwards with her own money. "But, hang on—" I began, "I didn't think we had enough for these."

"Well, I didn't exactly pay, as such," she mumbled.

"WHAT?!" I yelled.

She just giggled. "All right, Han! Don't have a heart attack! It's no big deal."

"Oh my God, Ellie!" I hissed. "You stole them. And you put them in my bag! Is that why you got me to go to the counter and ask if they had any more silver glitter gel? To keep that assistant distracted?"

"Yes," said Ellie, matter-of-factly, "and because I did want to know if they had any."

I felt awful – the shop lady had been so nice and helpful that I'd ended up telling her about the photo frames and my room and everything. And while we were having this nice chat, Ellie was shoplifting! "I can't believe you did that!" I cried. "If we'd been caught, I could have been arrested!"

Ellie squinted at me. "But that's why I put them in your bag, Han," she said patiently, like I was being a bit dim. "You'd have only got a warning, at your age, probably, but they'd have called the police on me if I'd done it."

I felt like banging my head on the table. "But you did do it!"

She sighed. "They wouldn't have known that, though. Anyway, why does it matter?" She grinned then. "Are you going to grass me up?"

"No, course not, but—" I stammered, my mind whirring. I felt sick and trembly. "Maybe you can put them back and no one will know. I'll come with you and—"

But she cut me off. "Han, honestly, relax. We spent loads in there and they mark up the prices so much in those posh shops anyway. They're probably only worth about 50p or something. I just really wanted to surprise you."

"Well, you certainly did that!" I shrieked. "I could be in a police cell right now!"

"Shhh!" She looked nervously at the door. It was the first time she'd seemed remotely worried. I knew why – if Mum found out about this she'd be on the next train back to Paris. "Look, I didn't realize a little thing like that would bother you," she said, finally taking it seriously. "I won't do it again, not now I know you mind so much."

"Good!" I hissed. Then after a moment I sighed and added, "Look, you didn't get caught, so I guess there's no point risking trouble by going back to the shop."

"Thanks, Han," she said. "And I really am sorry I upset you. I didn't mean to."

I sighed. "That's okay. Let's forget it, yeah?"

I mean, crazy or what?! I can hardly believe that

happened! And how casual she was about it. It's like she really didn't *get* what my problem was. But she seems to understand now, and she's not going to do it again, which is the main thing. She was just trying to do something nice for me, and I didn't want to upset her by going on about how she got them, or refusing to use them. So, even though I still felt bad, we stuck the flowers on the top corners of our frames. They were the perfect finishing touch.

When Dad came in we showed him the frames and he said how fab he thought they were and also that we were ultra-talented. Oh, I just thought, I forgot to mention his change, and Ellie must have, because she didn't give it to him. Oh well, he'll have to have it tomorrow now.

Mum said our frames were nice as well, but then she got all bustly like last night and made us clear up all the stuff and wipe the glue off the table. Then I had to set out while Ellie went upstairs to put the craft stuff out of the way.

And, oh dear, speaking of Mum, I think I upset her a bit tonight. I didn't mean to, but what happened was, we'd all been watching this show about terrible restaurants where the food tastes vile and you get poisoning from old dirty cloths and stuff. Ellie found it even *more* completely disgusting than we did and she was saying how no restaurant in France would ever be that filthy. Even though it was horrible to watch, it was really fun all going "Urgh! Gross!" together and shrieking.

Anyway, when it finished, Ellie just said goodnight and went upstairs to read in her room. I said I felt like reading in my room too. Mum said her usual, "I'll be up soon to tuck you in," and I didn't want to look like a baby so I said, "No need, I'll be fine by myself."

Mum looked really astonished, and not in a Hooray, Hannah is getting more independent type way but in an Oh. Hannah doesn't need me any more type way. Of course I didn't want to hurt her feelings, but then, she can't keep tucking me in for ever. I mean, when I'm at Uni she's not going to turn up every day and do it, is she? I pretended not to notice she was a bit upset and headed up here, cos it was easier than talking about it.

Oh, hang on…

2 mins later

Mum just came in to tell me to stop writing and turn my light off, so she did tuck me in after all. It was nice actually, because it felt a bit weird just going to bed without her coming up – kind of lonely. And Ellie didn't see her do it, which is the main thing.

Oh no, Mum's just stuck her head back round the door and said, "I am serious about lights out, Hannah!"

So, goodnight!

Wednesday before school
Can you believe how unfair Mum is being?!

You know how Ellie wears loads of bracelets all up her arm? Well, I really love that look, so this morning I tipped out my jewellery box, rolled up my shirtsleeves and put all mine on. I even wound some necklaces round my wrist to make it seem like I had a few more. It looked really nice even though it felt a bit heavy, but when I got downstairs, Mum sighed and said, "Hannah, don't even think about going to school like that."

Doh! I should have rolled my sleeves back down and put my jumper on so she didn't see. I was like, "Ellie wears hers to school," and Mum went all tight-lipped and said, "Yes, well, I'll have to have a word with your father about that too."

I hope Ellie won't be annoyed with me if she has to stop wearing them now. If that happens I'll tell her it's actually Mum's fault, which it is. I wish Mum wasn't so uptight and strict all the time. I bet when Ellie wore her bracelets like that to school in Paris her mum just said how clever she was for putting such a funky look together. Everyone's trendy in Paris. Mum should be happy we've got someone as stylish as Ellie in our family. Maybe Ellie could help her make over her frumpy wardrobe. Well, I don't mean frumpy exactly, but all she ever wears is black trousers with these V-neck jumpers that are exactly the same as each other but in different colours. She could do with a change.

Got to go – Mum's turfing us out the door.

Wednesday before tea, in my room

You won't believe what happened after lunch today. My heart starts pounding again if I even think about it. Well, I was late going outside because I had to change my library books. Afterwards I was wandering round by the netball courts looking for Maya and Beth when I spotted Ellie going down the little path behind the lunch hall (she hasn't got her uniform yet so she really stands out in all her bright colours).

I thought she didn't know we weren't allowed round there, because of being new. I didn't want her to get in trouble, so I cut across the playground and went after her, thinking I could just explain what I was doing if anyone stopped me. I went round the corner by the bushy bit at the back of the kitchen, where all the extractor fans are, and what I saw made me stop dead.

There was Ellie, with Jed and Cara. "Got this off Jimbo," she said to them.

"Nice one," Jed replied, cupping his hands close to hers. Then there was the click of a lighter and the crackle and flare of a cigarette. I made a sound by accident and they all whirled around.

When they saw me, Jed swore loudly (he'd thrown the fag in the bush) and Cara giggled.

"Jeez, Han, we thought you were a teacher!" cried Ellie. "What's up?"

I just shrugged, but I was thinking, *Duh, Hannah, obviously Ellie is already aware that they aren't allowed round here.*

Cara scrabbled around for the fag and puffed on it a bit to get it going again. Then she handed it to Ellie, who took a long drag then gave it back to Jed.

I tore my eyes away from the cigarette and forced myself to look casual. But I mean, smoking?! Are they crazy?! Don't they know about lung cancer?! But I didn't say any of that, of course. Instead I acted like it was normal.

"So, what's up, Han?" Ellie prompted.

"Oh, I, it's, er——" I was just trying to think of something to say when Jed offered me the cigarette.

Cara giggled again. "No way! She's well young."

My heart was thumping. I looked at Ellie. I thought she'd tell Jed not to be an idiot. But instead she just stood there, arms folded, watching me. Then she said, "Go on, Han, what are you scared of?" like it was no big deal.

Yes, it was stupid, but before I knew it, I'd taken the cigarette off Jed, put it to my lips and sucked. I guess I didn't want to look like a baby in front of Ellie's friends.

I coughed and spluttered as smoke puffed out of my nose, and for a moment I doubled over, really thinking I was going to be sick, or pass out.

They all laughed at first. But then Ellie stopped and gave Jed a shove and said, "Don't dis my sis."

She doesn't say stuff like that at home. And they

stopped laughing just like *that*, like she was the boss. Then Cara asked, "You okay, Han?"

I nodded, cos I still couldn't speak.

The bell went.

Nobody moved.

Ellie took the cigarette off Jed and finished it herself, without offering it round to them again, then ground it out under her boot. The way Jed watched her do it – well, he fancied her, you could tell.

Still no one moved.

"Erm, we should go in," I stuttered, finally feeling my lungs clear.

Ellie smiled at me. "Sure. You go ahead, we'll be in in a sec."

So I did.

See what I mean? What a crazy thing to happen.

I was still a bit freaked out about it when I met Ellie at the gate to walk home, and I was going to say something about how mad she is to smoke, but straight away she was herself again, talking normally, going, "I'm so sorry about that, Han. I can't *believe* Jed! What an idiot. Thanks for going along with it, though. You're so cool. My mates think so too."

I couldn't help feeling a bit pleased about that, so I

didn't go on to her about lung cancer in the end. Yeah, okay, so I had been a bit annoyed with her – I mean, I wished she'd stopped Jed in the first place, but she did stand up for me when they laughed, and anyway, it's my fault I tried it, not hers. I know I should have said no, but it's over now, there's no point worrying about it, and it was so vile there's no way I'll be doing it again! Just then Mr. Sharma, one of the science teachers, came out, and Ellie hurried me off, saying, "Whoops! Better go! I can't let him see me. Me and Jed kind of never made it back in after lunch. I got Cara to say I'd gone to a counselling appointment."

As she herded me through the gate, I tried to act normal, like it didn't shock me that she'd bunked off all afternoon, even though there's no way I'd ever do it.

"So what were you doing instead?" I asked, and then instantly felt stupid when she just raised an eyebrow.

"Ellie!" I squealed.

She giggled. "Well, Jed might be beyond dim, but he's a good kisser and he always has money on him. Oh, but don't say anything to Cara, though. They're kind of together."

I gasped. "Ellie! She's your mate!"

She nudged me playfully. "Don't look so serious, Han! It's only a casual thing between those two. She'll probably be with someone else next week, or maybe I will. There's no point me telling her and spoiling things – like you said, she's a mate."

"No, course not," I said. The way Ellie put it, it seemed like she was being thoughtful by not saying anything. Somehow I'd ended up looking like a boring old nag, acting like Cara and Jed were married or something. I didn't want Ellie to see me that way, so I got her chatting about whether she liked anyone else at school, and which actors and musicians she fancied.

It was great, me and my big sister having a girly chat about boys. And as we sat on a bench eating chips (which we bought with Dad's change, cos Ellie said she was sure he'd meant us to just have the whole twenty quid) I even ended up telling her my totally secret secret that I fancy Tom. When I said no way would he even look at me, she gave me a smile and said, "Course he would. You're gorgeous, Han. You just need a bit of make-up to bring your eyes out; that navy blue uniform makes you so pale. If he saw you when you're dressed up to go out, he wouldn't be able to **stop** looking at you." It made me feel all warm and glowy inside when she said that. And I loved the way she just assumed I get dressed up and go out, like a proper teenager, when I never do. Perhaps if I got invited to Anna's party... But nothing's been mentioned so far. I'll just have to keep saying bye to her at the gate, and chatting to Jecca and Nadia, and perhaps I'll get an invite at the last minute. You never know, miracles do happen. Not that I'd have anything to wear. There isn't one single glam thing in my wardrobe. Hey, I've just thought – maybe I'll find something like one of Ellie's cool dresses when we go round the shops on Saturday, so I can start a decent clothes collection!

Just writing this before
I turn my light out

I wanted to quickly say that Ellie had a call on her mobile as we were finishing our fruit salad. She went into the hallway and was speaking in her fast French so I knew it was the hospital again. I tried to listen in, but Mum told me not to be a nosy parker, then shut the kitchen door. When Ellie came back in there were tears in her eyes and she just looked at Dad and shook her head. He went and put his arm round her and said, "Never mind, love. I'm sure she's desperate to speak to you herself, but she's just not well enough."

I put my arm round her too and said, "Yeah. It won't be long, you'll see."

"Thanks, Han," she mumbled.

"Well, I might tackle those weeds on the patio," Dad said. "Fancy giving me a hand, Ellie?"

She nodded sadly. "I could help too," I offered, but Dad said, "No, you're all right, love," and they went out the back door. So I was left there with Mum but we didn't say anything to each other about Ellie. She started making the sandwiches for tomorrow and I came up here to write in this diary. I don't know why Dad thinks they can't talk about Celeste in front of me – I'm not a baby. I'm not going to be shocked – I've seen it all on Casualty. I wish I hadn't promised him not to talk to Ellie about it all now. There's so much I'd like to ask and I really think I could help her feel better. I'm way more understanding of emotions and stuff than he is.

Still, I'm sure Ellie will talk to me herself when she's ready – we're getting closer all the time, so she'll probably open up soon, and then we'll stay up, like, all night talking about her feelings and I'll listen really carefully and say loads of wise stuff and we'll have a sisterly hug and she'll say, Thank goodness I've got you, Han. There's no way I could get through this without you, and I'll say, No worries. That's what sisters are for.

Thursday –
oh dear, things have NOT gone very well today

The day started off badly when Ellie said she didn't want to go to school. Mum was in a rush trying to find her hairbrush, because she was going to be late for work, and she just said, "That's not how it works, young lady," in this really snappy way without even trying to make light of it. It's the first time she's said anything horrible to Ellie straight out like that. I gave her a don't-be-mean look but she didn't notice, or at least she pretended not to.

Then after school I waited for ages by the gate until nearly everyone had gone but Ellie still didn't come out. I tried her mobile but it just went to voicemail. Even if she had to stay behind for something I thought she would have popped out and told me, or texted. So I had to walk home on my own. It wasn't that big a deal that she didn't show up, but Mum was really off about it and she rang

Ellie's phone loads of times, but got her voicemail too. Ellie didn't get in till past six-thirty, when we were all in the middle of having our chicken wrapped in Parma ham (my request!). She came in all happy saying she'd stayed on to go to netball club with Cara and she thought she might even have a chance of getting in the school team. Dad said, "That's great, love," but instead of being pleased for her, Mum got all annoyed, saying how worried she'd been because Ellie hadn't told her where she was.

Ellie looked really confused and turned to me. "But Han, why didn't you tell them I was doing netball?" she asked.

I just sat there staring at her, totally stunned. She hadn't told me anything about it! I was just about to say that, when I realized she wanted me to cover for her. So of course I did. I couldn't let her down, or get her into trouble with Mum. "Oh, yeah," I mumbled. "Sorry, I forgot you'd said that." I had to concentrate really hard on staying relaxed so my face didn't go bright red.

"Hannah!" Mum cried. "How could you just forget when I've been standing here in front of you calling Ellie's phone and worrying!"

"I'm sorry, I just did," I mumbled, staring at the table.

Mum made an annoyed kind of tutting sound, then she turned to Ellie and did her *exasperated* look – the same one she gives me when I use up the OJ and then put the empty carton back in the fridge. "You need to ring me next time," she said crossly. "It seems that you can't rely on Hannah to pass on messages. I was so concerned about you."

"Sorry," Ellie muttered, "I thought telling Hannah would be okay."

Mum and Ellie both looked really upset then and I didn't know what to say. My head was still reeling about getting into trouble for something I didn't even do! But luckily Dad stepped in. "Just give Charlotte a quick ring or a text next time, love," he told Ellie cheerily. "We know how old you are, but she's not used to having teens around and you don't want her to worry."

Ellie nodded, but Mum gave Dad a look like he'd put *ten* empty OJ cartons back in the fridge. Then she got Ellie's dinner out of the oven with loads of banging around, and Ellie ate it really quickly and went straight to her room without saying anything to anyone, not even me. Poor thing. I wish Mum would try to make more of an effort with her. When I went upstairs, Ellie came into my room and said, "Oh, Han, I'm so sorry about that. I didn't even think of ringing Charlotte until just now when she said something, and then I was so worried about getting into trouble, especially after she was so off with me this morning, I just said the first thing that came into my head. Thanks so much for going along with it."

I was going to say how annoying it was standing by the gate on my own until everyone had gone, and that I'd been worried about her too, but I thought that might make me sound like a really boring old nag again, so I didn't. Instead I said, "No problem."

She smiled. "You're so great, Han, I really appreciate it."

Well, that made me feel all lit up inside. Ellie gave me a hug and I hugged her back and found myself coming out with those magic words I've been wanting to say. "That's what sisters are for."

And then, even better, she said, "Yeah. Cheers, l'il sis." It was one of the nicest moments I've ever had and I'm going to remember it for ever. It probably would have led to us talking about the car accident and how Ellie's mum is now and everything, if Ellie hadn't gone off to have a bath.

Oh, hang on – something's going on downstairs. I think Mum and Dad are having a row.

I was right. It went on for about half an hour, but now Dad's slammed out of the front door and Mum's crying in the kitchen. I feel really sick and trembly, because I don't know what to do. I should go down there – but it'll be really awkward and I won't know what to say. Maybe I'll just go and give her a hug. But then she'll know I've heard and I shouldn't really have been earwigging. Maybe I should stay put and give her some space. She might not want me to see her in such a state. Oh, I don't know! Maybe I'll give it a little while and then go down. Yes, okay, I'll do that.

Thank goodness Ellie didn't hear them. I was sitting on the top step and as her door was open a crack I could see her reflected in her new mirror. She was lying on her bed in her dressing gown with her eyes shut listening to her iPod the whole time. Maybe she'd know what to say to Mum if I asked her, but I don't want to have to explain that the row was about *her*. Then she'd be upset too, when none of this is her fault.

I can't remember the whole argument, not *exactly*, but after a lot of banging and crashing, which was Mum doing the washing-up in an angry way, Dad asked what was wrong. Then Mum started saying she felt like Dad had undermined her when Ellie came in tonight. That's when I put this notebook down and leaped off my bed and ran into the hall so I could listen properly. Dad said it wasn't a big deal, and how Ellie's a teenager not a little kid. "She needs to have more freedom than Hannah," he added, "and she hasn't learned our rules and boundaries yet."

Mum said, "Yes, well, it looks like she's never learned *any* rules and boundaries." I remember that bit exactly, because I could just imagine her pursing her lips after she'd said it.

Dad said, "You'll have to start letting go more anyway, with Hannah getting older. She'll be like Ellie soon enough."

Mum got really cross then and said that me and Ellie are *nothing* like each other, and I got the feeling she wanted to add *thank goodness*. That made me feel so annoyed with her. Why does she have to make things difficult? Everything's going brilliantly. Why can't she just cheer up and join in? And anyway, I can't think of anything *better* than being like Ellie!

Then Mum said something strange, which was, "It's not fair that I'm expected to look after Ellie but I have no say in how she's handled."

That's when I realized that she must feel like she can't just *say* something to Ellie about stuff like wearing the bracelets and mucking around at the table because Ellie's not her daughter. I hadn't thought about that before. But anyway, like Dad said, there won't be any problems as soon as Ellie learns how not to upset Mum.

"Oh, Charlotte, of course you have a say," Dad said, like Mum was being ridiculous. I thought that would be the end of it – after all, that's what they were arguing about, wasn't it? But instead Mum just seemed to get even more annoyed.

"Well then, back me up!" she yelled, so loud I would have heard her even if I hadn't been earwigging. "It's not easy for me, you know! I can't believe you've been such a soft touch. This woman just contacts you out of the blue—"

Dad cut in. "Not Celeste, Ellie," he corrected, which made Mum even more annoyed.

"Well, okay, so Ellie tracked you down from what Celeste told her," she hissed. "Same difference. When she needs help, when it suits her, she reveals that you're the father! This woman didn't think you had the right to know you had a child for fifteen years and then suddenly she dumps Ellie on you and you just go…" Mum put on a stupid voice, "duh. Okay."

That was when Dad got really cross. "She's my daughter!" he shouted.

And my sister! I wanted to add. I was glad he wasn't backing down. Like he said before, Ellie is family – I don't know why Mum's being so difficult about it. It's only for a few precious months at most. Doesn't she want us all to be happy together while we can?

"I wasn't given the chance to do the right thing by her before so it's even more important that I do it now," Dad said, well, shouted. "She wasn't dumped on me. It's a pleasure to have her here. And as for Celeste, I can't believe you can be so unkind! After what she's been through, with the accident—"

Mum did a kind of snort of laughter thing that was definitely NOT because she found anything funny. "Oh, don't play that card, Sam!" she hissed. "You know I sympathize with Celeste's situation. It's just – the nerve of the woman. The presumption. She gave *no* thought to how this would affect our lives."

Dad was really furious by then. "I told you, Ellie's—"

I heard his fist bang down on the table. To me, the silence afterwards was louder than the shouting.

When he spoke again, he just sounded really tired and fed up. "Oh, never mind, Charlotte," he said. "I'm sick of going round in circles. I give up. Whatever I say seems to be wrong."

Then I heard footsteps in the hall, and I ducked back in here, but no one came up. Instead there was a jangle of car keys being lifted from the hook. Mum shouted, "Fine! Just brush it all under the carpet – like you always do! Just keep telling yourself everything's okay!"

But Dad didn't say anything back. Instead, the door slammed shut.

Oh, I wish they could just sort it out – I hate them fighting, it makes me feel like I did when I thought they were splitting up. I have to find a way to bring Mum round, or everything could be ruined. If Ellie doesn't feel welcome she might want to go back to Paris, and then I'll lose my fabulous sister when I've only just found her.

Oh no, I just went down to see Mum but she must have slipped off to bed while I was writing this, so I'd better not disturb her now.

Friday after tea

Just to say quickly that Dad came back at about 11.30 last night and, although things were a bit frosty between him and Mum before they left for work this morning, it seemed okay at tea. Thank goodness, because I was getting really worried about them. And I didn't want Maya and Beth to notice any tension when they come round tomorrow.

No party invite from Anna, sadly. I did look for her at the gate – I thought maybe if I said something like, *Have fun tomorrow night*, she might ask me along, and Maya and Beth too, but she wasn't around and nor were Jecca and Nadia. Oh well, I guess I won't be wowing Tom this weekend, then! (As if I could anyway! I just got caught up in Ellie's imagination for a while there!)

Saturday

Today went brilliantly, well, apart from this one thing, but me and Ellie have sorted that out now. And something really extra exciting has happened too! I'm just sitting on my bed writing this while waiting for Mum and Dad to get back from Waitrose. I hope they hurry up, because—

No, hang on, I'll go back to the beginning and make myself say everything in order.

Okay, so, when Beth and Maya arrived I took them straight up to see my new room (me and Ellie finished it off last night with the pinboard full of fashion pix and it looks fab!). Beth absolutely loved it and Maya asked where we got the big flower picture from. Ellie made ice cream sundaes using strawberry sauce and all the flavours that were in the freezer (choc, vanilla and tutti-frutti) and brought them upstairs to us.

We drew the curtains so we could put on my flamingo fairy lights and all four of us sat on the purple spirally rug by my bed eating our ice cream and chatting. It was fab, like a daytime sleepover! Of course, Maya (and Beth!) thought Ellie was completely fantastic. They were both saying how much they liked her dress and her bracelets and her make-up, and, well, everything about her. When Ellie said she liked Maya's eye-shimmer gel, she looked really, really pleased and Beth looked kind of jealous – hee hee! Then Ellie told them about sneaking into a nightclub in Paris with some older friends and they were both so impressed. Maya told her about going to that gig with Radha and I could tell Beth was wishing she had something like that to say as well.

Then, as me and Ellie had planned all along, I casually suggested heading into town. Beth wrinkled up her nose at me and said, "Will your dad let us, though?" and it was so cool when I got to say, "Yeah, course," like I didn't even know why she'd asked. She was really surprised!

Then Ellie acted like she just fancied coming along with us, saying she needed to get some more eyeliner anyway, so they didn't guess she had to be there. While she was putting her boots on, I popped into the garden to say goodbye to Mum and Dad to make sure they didn't come to the door and say anything that would give the game away. It was so much fun just having a secret between me and Ellie – the others had no idea they'd completely fallen for our plan!

In town, we looked round the shops for a bit, and we all tried some stuff on in Miss Selfridge, but there was nothing we liked enough to buy. Then we had a wander down a little cobbledy street and went in this place called Head in the Clouds. I'd never noticed it before but Ellie spotted it straight away. They had loads of gorgeous crystals and multi-coloured jackets made out of felt. There was also some of that stuff I find a bit spooky like tarot cards and skull-shaped candles, but I just tried not to look at it. Ellie bought some incense sticks and a dreamcatcher to hang over her bed, and of course Beth and Maya copied her and got one each too. I bought this cool wrist band made from braided green leather. I've decided I'm going to get as many bracelets as Ellie but just add them one by one so

Mum doesn't notice. Good thinking, huh?!

After that we were all getting hungry but we'd spent most of our money in Head in the Clouds, so I said, "Let's see how much we've got and maybe we can scrape enough together to share a portion of chips."

But Ellie just grinned and unzipped the pocket on her leather jacket. She did a sort of magician's flourish with her fingers and pulled out a twenty-pound note. "Daddy dearest is treating us all to lunch," she announced.

"Wow!" cried Beth. "Cool!"

"Yeah, he is really cool, our dad," said Ellie. "He paid for everything for Hannah's room, and helped us do the painting and bought us loads of art stuff. He'll do anything for us girls."

It took me by surprise at first. Her saying "daddy dearest" and "our dad". It felt a bit weird, but I liked it. And "us girls". Me and Ellie. Ellie and me. Sisters.

Beth started doing that dance off the telly, swaying her hips and swinging her arms and singing, "Go Ellie! Go Ellie!" Maya joined in and then I did too. Then I realized that I'd done it without feeling shy or self-conscious, just because I'd been enjoying myself so much. At that moment it really felt like we were a three and not just like they were a two with me tagging on. Ellie's plan was working brilliantly.

Beth suggested McDonald's and I was about to go *yeah!* but the look on Ellie's face made that idea seem instantly uncool so I did the same look at Beth too. "I know where we can get something much better than that," Ellie said. "Come on!"

She linked arms with me and set off running, like we were going on a magical mystery tour. With Beth and Maya hanging on to our sleeves and all four of us giggling, we ran back down the hill and Ellie steered us into the market and over to this hotdog stall. They were proper banger-type sausages, not those Americany ones. They came in French bread and we put on loads of ketchup and mayo as well, all mixed together. When Beth and Maya were up at the counter getting more napkins, Ellie said to me, "Oh, Han, I almost forgot. Dad didn't give me the twenty quid *as such*, so maybe don't mention it to him, yeah? I just took it out of his wallet when I made the ice creams."

I must have looked a bit shocked because she added, "I would have asked him if he'd been there, you know I would. And he would have been fine with it."

I felt really muddled then, like I couldn't think properly. True, he probably would have given her the money, but that wasn't the point. It was still stealing. Or perhaps it wasn't, so long as she mentioned it when we got back? "I – er – Ellie, I don't think..." I began, but, "Oh, come on, Han," she said, sighing, "I only did it for you, so we could treat your mates to lunch and really impress them. And it worked. You saw Beth's reaction."

Luckily I realized how uptight I was being then, and how ungrateful. I smiled and went, "Yes, course, it was a great idea. Thanks, Ellie."

Thank goodness I turned that around before she started thinking I was a complete sad case. I feel bad about not acting cooler at the time, though. That's the thing about Ellie, she's laid-back, chilled out. She doesn't make a big fuss over silly little things like I do. I wish I was more like her. I mean, what was I thinking? She wouldn't steal from Dad. Of course she'll tell him about the money when they get in from Waitrose. She said herself that the only reason she didn't before was because he wasn't there, and she must have forgotten when she popped out to the garden to say goodbye.

It was great, us four sitting in the sunshine, munching our hotdogs and slurping from cans of Coke. "How do you know about this place?" I asked Ellie after a while. "I didn't think you'd been into town yet."

She grinned at me and wiped her chin with a paper napkin. "That netball practice I told your mum I'd been to was actually at lunchtime," she said. "The real reason I was late back the other night was cos me, Cara and Jed came down here to hang out after school. I just told a little fib to save Charlotte getting in a tizz – even though she kind of did anyway." She rolled her eyes and Maya and Beth giggled.

I made myself smile although I got a funny feeling in my stomach hearing that. Well, of course I know Mum gets tizzy, but it's not nice to hear it said out loud. And I wish Ellie hadn't lied to her, but I suppose I can understand why she did. I mean, look what a big deal Mum made about her being late, even after Ellie had told her that she'd been at netball practice. She would have been much worse if she'd known Ellie had actually been hanging around town with her friends, eating hotdogs right before dinner. I do wish she had told me the real truth, though – I would have kept it quiet.

Anyway, we were all nearly finished and Ellie said, "Right, what do you feel like doing next?"

I was going to suggest walking down to that surfy-type shop at the bottom of the high street when Beth said, "We could go and hang round the skatepark," and did a big wink at me. I instantly went as red as the ketchup on my hotdog, even before Maya added, "Yeah, Hannah, maybe Tom will be there."

"So what if he is?" I managed to mumble. "It's not like I care."

Maya giggled. "Yeah, right."

"We've seen you staring at him in the lunch queue," Beth teased.

"Not cos I fancy him!" I said lamely, but my face had gone so bright red it was obvious I really did. Not that there's any point in liking him. He'd never like me back, not in a million years, because he's cool and skater-y and only hangs round with girls like Jecca and Nadia.

"You so fancy him," Beth insisted, while I went

even redder and started to wonder if my face might catch fire.

Then the horrible thing that happened happened.

We saw Anna from 8W and her friend Chloe, and they said hi, and we all said hi back. I waited for Beth to chat to them, cos she's always the one who takes the lead out of us three, but she just looked a bit flustered and fiddled with the key rings on her bag. Then Maya said something about all their shopping bags and Chloe pulled out this top to show us, that she'd got for Anna's party. "Anyway, better go, see y'all tonight, girlies!" Anna said then. "Beth told me you can come, yeah?"

"Yeah, that's right. Thanks for inviting us. Cool," Beth mumbled.

"Laters," said Chloe, and off they went.

Well, me, Maya and Ellie were all staring at Beth. "What's going on?" I asked. I had an uneasy feeling even though I hadn't exactly worked it all out, not by then. But Beth was silent.

"I don't get it, Beth," Maya said. "You told me it was only us two who'd been invited. But Anna just said *all* of us."

My stomach did a huge flip and, for a moment,

I thought I was going to throw up my hotdog. "What?" I gasped. "You two were going without me?"

Maya looked really flustered and upset then. So she should, I thought, feeling my face go red hot. "I did tell Beth we shouldn't go at all if you weren't invited," she mumbled. "But she's got this new top she wants to wear, so..."

"Huh!" I snorted. I mean, isn't that the most rubbish excuse *ever*?

I gave Maya a killer glare. Beth was staring blankly into space and wouldn't look at either of us. It was so obvious – she'd lied to Maya so she could go to the party with just her, and not me. I felt so angry about that, and really ashamed too. "Maya, Beth made up that thing about only you and her being invited so she could leave me out. Can't you see that?" I demanded.

Then I glared at Beth, and so did Ellie. "Is that true?" Maya asked, a tremor in her voice. "Beth?"

Beth was still staring vacantly, then suddenly she came to life. She let out a high, fake laugh, then turned on me. "Chill out, Han!" she shrilled. "Don't be so paranoid! Course I didn't do that! Anna did only invite us two. I even asked her if you could come but she changed the subject, so I thought I should drop it. Seeing you sitting right here in front of her just now, well, she must have felt awkward about it and invited you on the spot."

I gave her a dirty look, then turned to Maya. "Surely you don't believe that?" I muttered. I fully expected her to understand what Beth had been up to. But, unbelievably, she still looked uncertain.

"Come on, Maya, think about it," I cried. "I'm the only one out of us three who Anna's ever spoken to. If only I'd seen her around the last couple of days, she would have mentioned my invite before now. Beth must have been so pleased when school ended yesterday, thinking she'd got away with keeping it from me!"

"I did not!" Beth shrieked.

I really believed Maya would tell Beth how out of order she was, and maybe even break friends with her. But she just peered back at me and said, "Oh, Han, why would she do something like that to you when we're all mates? Anna must have changed her mind just now, like Beth said."

Beth gave me a nasty sneer and I felt like

screaming. Maya had been totally brainwashed! That was it – official – my best mate had abandoned me! I felt so ashamed I couldn't even look at Ellie – she'd think I was a total loser after this.

But then I felt her hand squeeze mine under the table. "Sounds like you *were* all invited from the start, but you must have misunderstood Anna," she said to Beth. "I'm sure you didn't *mean* to leave Hannah out, not deliberately."

Beth stared at her for a minute. So did I! At first I was thinking, What?! How can she believe Beth too?! But then I realized what she was doing. Of course she didn't believe Beth, but she knew Maya did. She knew that if me and Beth broke up over it, Maya would choose *her*. By giving Beth a way out, Ellie was saving me, too.

Beth was silent for a moment, probably weighing up her options. Then she mumbled, "Yeah, I suppose I could have got it wrong, but I really thought she said only us two."

"Well, you obviously misheard," said Ellie briskly. "Oh, well, never mind. Luckily the muddle has been sorted out in time so no harm done. Let's all move on, yes?"

"Sorry for getting mixed up, Hannah," said Beth, with a face like she was sucking a lemon.

"S'okay," I managed to mutter.

"Oh, please say you'll come, Han," Maya cried suddenly. "If you don't I'll feel awful about it for *ever*."

It made me feel a bit better, having Maya beg me like that. I shrugged and said, "Okay, whatever," trying to make it sound like I didn't care either way.

"Fantastic," said Maya, sounding relieved.

"Cool," mumbled Beth.

"Good," said Ellie.

When Beth and Maya were taking the paper plates and cans to the bin, me and Ellie shared a secret smile. That was amazing, the way she'd turned things round, so that Beth could save face and I could still go to the party with them. I do wish Maya had believed me, though. It really hurts that she didn't.

When I suggested going to the surfy-type shop, everyone agreed that it was a good idea. Beth was obviously trying to prove that she had nothing against me and that she hadn't lied. I didn't even mind too much when Maya and Beth got the bus together, cos

I felt like having Ellie to myself by then, and I'm seeing them again tonight anyway. Me and Ellie chatted all the way home about what a little liar Beth is, and how cool the party'll be. Ellie's going to help me get ready too – I didn't find anything new out shopping today, but she says she'll lend me some of her stuff. How amazing is that – to actually wear some of Ellie's cool gear!

Oh, that's Mum and Dad back from Waitrose, I'll go and tell them about the party now. I wish they'd got back sooner, I mean, it starts at seven and it's six now, but if I hurry I can probably still get ready in time. Ellie's going to do my make-up too! I can't wait!

6.30 p.m.

Can you believe it?! I should be setting off for the party soon, but instead I'm lying on my bed writing this, just wanting to SCREAM with frustration!!!

So, Mum and Dad came in and I went downstairs to tell them the fabulous news that I had been lucky enough to be invited to the coolest party of Year 8 so far, and that we needed to set off to Anna's house in only about 45 minutes. Ellie had remembered to get Anna's address from Beth, luckily, not that it matters now, because Dad said NO to me going!

Unbelievable!

In fact what he said was, "Hannah, this is very short notice, we've only just got in the door and you expect me to go straight back out again and then come out again to pick you up."

"I'm sorry but it's just not on, Hannah," said Mum as she unloaded the vegetables into the fridge.

That's when Ellie wandered in and pulled a bunch of bananas from one of the shopping bags, snapped one off and started unpeeling it. Mum did her not-just-before-dinner frown but she didn't say anything.

I sighed. "It's not my fault I didn't know before now, it's Beth's," I explained. "Anyway, it's not that far away, just out of town on that new estate by the big cinema and bowling place, and it finishes at ten so it's not exactly late." I did try my best not to sound annoyed at them but I couldn't help it. Why didn't they understand how important this was? "Everyone wanted to go to this party, and I've been invited," I cried. "And Maya and Beth are going."

"Well, good for them, but I'm afraid Mum and I have already made plans," Dad said firmly. "We've got a table booked at Milanos for seven, and we're going on to The Belvedere afterwards. We're getting taxis into town and back so we can both have a drink. I'm not missing out on that just to play chauffeur to you all night."

"Well, maybe we could see if Sita can collect her," Mum suggested. "It's out of her way, but—"

"She can't!" I cried, feeling really frustrated. "Maya's going with Beth's mum on the way there, with Nadia and Jecca too, and Jecca's dad's bringing them all back, so the cars are already full." Beth had really enjoyed telling me that this afternoon, she was almost more excited about sharing lifts with Jecca and Nadia than she was about the actual party.

"Well then you'll have to stay in," said Mum. "Your dad and I need some time together. It's been ages since we had a night out."

"Ellie'll be here to look after you, won't you, love?" Dad said. CRINGE! Like I need a babysitter or something!

"Yeah, but…I could take her down and pick her up," Ellie offered. What a star! But it was no use.

Dad just said, "That's very sweet of you, love, but I'm not having you walking around on your own at ten o'clock at night, especially not along that dual carriageway. Hannah's been out all day with her friends. She can just stay put tonight."

ARGH! "Excuse me, I am here, you know!" I cried.

Mum was on it like a shot. "Don't be so rude, young lady," she snapped. "Not everything revolves around you, you know. Now, I'll get these chicken kievs in the oven and Ellie can pop some vegetables on and serve up for you both."

After that I was just staring at them in disbelief! They actually really weren't going to take me to the party! Didn't they know they were ruining my life?! "So now Beth and Maya will hang round together without me all night, and then they'll be talking about it at school on Monday and I'll be left out and Beth'll take Maya away for good, so thanks very much!" I shouted, then stomped off up here.

"Hannah, don't be such a drama queen!" Mum called after me, but I didn't reply. They just came up to say goodbye though, and I had to speak to them or I'd have got told off for sulking. But I didn't let myself hug them goodbye, because then they might have thought that I don't mind about the party any more, when I DO!

Oh, Ellie's just come in.

I'm quickly scribbling this down

Well, there I was thinking Ellie had come up to say the food was ready (I mean, they don't even trust me to cook my own tea, like I'm going to burn the house down or something!), but instead she came dancing into the room and did a big flourish over me, like she was waving a magic wand, and cried, "Cinderella, you shall go to the ball!"

I just blinked at her, going, "What?"

She beamed at me, eyes twinkling. "I've rung Jed and Cara and they're up for the cinema, so I'll walk you to the party, then meet up with them and after the film I'll come and get you again. No problem."

I stared at her. "Really? You'd do that for me?"

Ellie grinned. "Course. That's what sisters are for, right?"

I smiled at that, then asked, "But what about us walking home so late? I suppose Dad did have a point about that."

Ellie giggled. "Han! Ten's not late! I used to walk about in Paris all the time completely on my own, way later than that..." She paused for a moment, her face clouding over. I was about to ask what was wrong, when she brightened again and carried on, saying, "I mean, when I was coming back from clubs and stuff. It's fine, honestly. And I'll cadge some cash off Jed anyway, so we can use a bit of that for a cab. Like I said, he's always got money."

It was a brilliant plan, but I still wasn't sure. I mean, I've never gone behind Mum and Dad's backs like that before. "What if—" I began, but Ellie cut me off, reading my mind. "They'll never know," she insisted. "By the time they get in from The Belvedere," she put on a snooty accent to say that, "you'll be tucked up in bed. But I'll leave a note to say we've gone to the cinema with my friends, and that Cara's mum's taking us there and bringing us home, so they won't worry about us walking. That way, if they do come back early for any reason, we've covered our backs."

I was going to say thanks, but no, I just couldn't do that when I knew I wasn't allowed to go. But then I thought, *What's the problem?* I'll either be with Ellie or at the party, so I'll be safe at all times, which is what they're actually worried about.

I have to go for it. If I don't, it'll ruin my chances of keeping in with Maya and Beth and they'll go off as a two, I just know it. Mum and Dad wouldn't want me to be miserable and lonely at school, would they? And anyway, why should I miss out just because they don't understand how important this is?

I turned to my fabulous sister and smiled nervously, "Okay," I said.

She smiled back at me. "Excellent. It'll be brilliant, Hannah. And like I said, you can borrow some of my stuff. Hey, I know, I'll give you a makeover. You'll look great, and you'll have the best time ever. Maya will be so impressed and Tom will probably ask you out!"

Wow! Ellie's going to wave her magic wand and make all my dreams come true. I felt absolutely glowing. I smiled back at my amazing big sister, who was about to give me a cool makeover so I could wow everyone at the party. Maybe even Tom. Maybe

I'll hang around with Jecca and Nadia, and only let Beth in if I'm feeling really, really kind. Or maybe me and Maya will end up sitting on the stairs having a really deep girly chat, just us two.

Any worries I had about Mum and Dad have vanished now. It's like they've been zapped by Ellie's magic wand. I'm so lucky to have her. Even though we've only known each other a little while, I feel like we've really connected. I'm so glad she's here, and that she's my sister.

Gotta go. Ellie's got herself ready now and she's about to start on me!

It's a miracle – I actually look nice!

Well, that's something I never thought I'd ever say! Somehow, Ellie has worked her magic again and I look cool and grown up, and even (I can't believe I'm writing this) a bit pretty!

She cut off some jeans of mine to make shorts (a pair I never wore cos they had weird patches of different denim sewn onto the knees – somehow Mum persuaded me they were nice in the shop).

I was a bit worried they were too short, but Ellie said they looked really good and, anyway, she's lent me some fab bright purple tights to go under them, which look amazing with her high-heeled boots. We had to shove tissue paper down the toes cos they were way too big for me, but I've had a practice walking now and I don't wobble, well, not that much.

She's also lent me her pink floaty-gauzy top – my fave out of all her stuff – and she's done my eye make-up the same as hers, except a bit stronger because it's a party and the lights will be down (good thinking by Ellie, I don't want to look washed out!). She added some pink lipstain too, to go with the top. It's a bit chilly for the walk up there, but luckily I can wear my long grey coat on top, all buttoned up to keep me warm.

I can't believe how old I look – at least 14, I reckon. Ellie says Tom will be blown away. I don't know about that, but, well, maybe! I did start worrying at one point about Mum and Dad somehow finding out, but I pushed those thoughts out of my mind. I want to be the new Hannah, the sparkly, grown-up, cool Hannah, not the old boring worrying one.

We'll be a bit late, I mean, it's already twenty past seven, but we had to eat and sort the kitchen out or Mum would have got suspicious, then Ellie said we ought to just leave it a bit longer to make sure they haven't forgotten something and end up coming back for it – she really thinks of everything! She says you should always be a bit late to a party anyway, so you can make an entrance. I can't wait to make mine and reveal the cool new Hannah – everyone's going to be totally stunned. Ellie really *can* make magic happen. I really *do* feel like Cinderella going to the ball!

Oh fab, we're ready to go now! I'm so nervous and excited! I have a feeling this is going to be the best night of my life so far!

Saturday night, huddled up in bed

I've only just stopped crying enough to be able to write this. So much for our perfect plan. I have never felt so embarrassed in my entire life. I can hardly bear to write down what happened. But I'll force myself to, because hopefully then it'll stop going round and round in my head.

When we arrived at Anna's, Maya and Beth made such a big deal, squealing loudly and hugging us both, probably so that everyone would see they knew Ellie. Even Tom turned round and smiled at me, and amazingly I managed not to go bright red, but to just smile back instead, like a normal person. I felt so proud to be with my sister, especially when she gave me a hug goodbye in front of everyone and whispered, "Knock 'em dead," in my ear. I really did feel like a whole new person.

But then I took off my coat, and everything went wrong.

I should have wondered why Maya hissed something to Beth, and Beth shushed her. But I was too excited about my big Cinderella-style entrance.

When we went through to the kitchen, Mrs. Szarko, Anna's mum, said, "Hello, dear. Hannah, isn't it?" She had a surprised expression on her face and of course I thought it was because she was wondering how I could be in Year 8 when I looked so grown up.

As I got some fruit punch and a sausage roll, I noticed some of the boys, including Tom, kind of nudging each other and sniggering, but I didn't know why. They're always acting immature so I didn't realize it was about me. But then when Mrs. Szarko went into the living room, Jecca said, "Nice outfit, Hannah, although it's not meant to be fancy dress," and Nadia laughed.

My cheeks burned and my knees buckled. Of course, I'd expected Maya to say how great I looked and tell Jecca to get lost, but she just stared into her punch and Beth said, "Well, I wasn't going to say anything, Han, but maybe it is a bit…you know."

I looked at Tom but he was kind of gazing through me, as if I was invisible. Jecca smirked at me and started talking to Nadia again. My heart was hammering and it really felt like my knees were going to give way at any second.

Just then I glanced back towards the front door and caught sight of myself in the hall mirror.

The heel of one of Ellie's borrowed boots had snagged my purple tights on the way here, and they'd laddered so badly I'd had to nip behind a bush and take them off. I'd wanted to go home and get some more, but Ellie would have missed the start of the film and anyway, she persuaded me that my legs looked fine. But now I saw that they didn't, not in the light. You couldn't see the denim shorts at all so I just looked half-dressed and my bare legs were blueish and mottled with cold.

And as for the rest of it – was this really the same outfit I'd *loved* so much back at home? Ellie's boots were way too big – they made me look like a little kid trying on her mum's shoes. The pink chiffony-gauzy top was so loose on me it had slipped off one shoulder. We'd had the lights low for getting ready, and I hadn't realized my ENTIRE bra showed through it. And now everyone had seen it, even the boys.

My heart raced and my stomach lurched. I hadn't been magically transformed into a cool new person. I was the same old me, but now I looked like a total idiot.

And right there, in front of everyone, I clamped my arms across my chest and burst into tears. Not stylish, jewel-like film star tears but big fat rolling drops. Mascara and eyeliner slid down my cheeks. Snot bubbled out of my nose, and I tried to run up to the bathroom, but in the too-big boots I could only hobble up the stairs slowly, hanging on to the banister, still trying to hide my bra with my other arm.

There. I've written it. Deep breath. No, it hasn't worked. I don't feel any better. I just cannot BELIEVE this has happened.

Once I got into the bathroom and locked the door, I slid to the floor and started crying. And I just couldn't stop. Maya tried to talk to me through the door, but there was no way I had anything to say to her, not after she'd betrayed me like that. She must have realized I looked awful as soon as I undid my coat – and I can't believe Beth stopped her from saying anything. Maya could easily have made me button it up again quick, then got Anna to lend me something to wear, but she let me take it off and completely embarrass myself instead.

Beth didn't even bother coming up the stairs after me – shows what kind of a friend she is! After Maya gave up, Mrs. Szarko tried to get me to come out too, but I wouldn't say a word to her either. Even if I'd wanted to, I couldn't have, because I just couldn't stop crying – I could hardly breathe, let alone speak.

Then something even worse happened.

A few minutes later Mrs. Szarko called in to me that she'd got my mum's mobile number from Maya's mum and that Dad was coming to get me. OMG! Their dinner had been ruined. Worse, they knew what I'd done. I was so scared, imagining how angry they'd be.

I managed to calm down a bit so I could call Ellie and warn her we were in deep trouble, but she didn't pick up. I didn't understand why, cos we'd promised to ring each other if there were any problems. I know she was in the cinema but that shouldn't have made any difference – she'd just have put her phone on vibrate. But it went straight to voicemail and I ended up leaving these sniffling, sobbing messages about what had happened. I thought about texting, but my hands were shaking too much.

When Dad arrived, I knew I had to come out, but I was still hoping I could just slip off into the car really fast and avoid everyone. No such luck. Instead, we all stood in the hallway for what felt like ages with loads of kids, including Tom, hovering in the doorway to the kitchen (I managed to grab my coat and get it on, at least). Mrs. Szarko said, "I don't know what happened, I'm afraid. Of course girls do fall out all the time, but Hannah was locked in the bathroom crying and she sounded so upset I thought I must ring you."

"Thank you so much," said Dad, in his forced-jolly voice. "Oh well, these things happen. Pre-teen girls – it's all a mystery to me."

They said their goodbyes and even though I was still really upset, Dad made me say "thank you for having me," to Anna and her mum. Of course, the adults were both politely acting like they hadn't noticed my outfit, but as soon as we got in the car

Dad went crazy. I don't want to write down exactly what he said, cos I'll just start crying again, but he was furious about the clothes, the make-up, and most of all that I'd gone to the party when they'd said no. "And we had to leave halfway through our starter," he fumed. "Your mum was so embarrassed, poor thing. And I've ended up driving you about after all. Lucky for you we'd hardly started on our bottle of wine. How could you do this, Hannah?" My heart was hammering and I felt really sick. I hardly dared look at him. I felt like a piece of rubbish on the pavement and tears started running down my face again.

"I saw Ellie's note about the cinema," Dad said then. "I've texted her to say I've got you, so Cara's mum can bring her straight home after the film. I assumed you cooked this plan up together?"

I didn't say anything to that. There's no way I'm going to land Ellie in it. We've got to look out for each other. That's what sisters are for. Instead I said, "Her phone's out of battery or something. She didn't pick up when I called her."

"Well, she texted *me* straight back," said Dad.

Strange. Perhaps the signal was a bit patchy in the

cinema. As we pulled into the drive, Dad said, "Now, when we get through that door I want you to get yourself upstairs, take that muck off your face and go straight to bed. Understand?"

"Yes," I mumbled.

And when we got in I bolted up here, still in my coat. I couldn't face seeing Mum and she must be really upset with me not to come up and say goodnight. I'm feeling sick just thinking of what she's going to say tomorrow. I quickly texted Ellie, seeing as Dad's message got through, to let her know I haven't said anything about it being her idea. We have to stick together on this. Then I got changed and cleaned off the make-up, brushed my teeth and got into bed. But I couldn't sleep, of course. I just lay here thinking – well – trying *not* to think. And when I'd calmed down enough I put my lamp on and started writing this. I don't—

Oh, I can hear a car pulling up outside (must be a cab cos, of course, Cara's mum wasn't actually picking us up), a door slamming, footsteps, and now that's Ellie's key in the door. I hope Dad's not too hard on her. I'm just going to creep to the stairs so I can hear what's going on.

Even now, I can hardly believe what's just happened.

It doesn't seem real.

It's hard to write this because my hands are shaking so much.

Ellie started talking as soon as she came in the door (Dad was there waiting for her). I couldn't believe what I was hearing. She asked him what had happened, like she didn't know. Like she hadn't got any messages from me. Like she'd never put me in that outfit, or come up with the whole idea.

When Dad told her what had happened, she acted all surprised. "Oh, Sam, I'm so sorry," she gasped. "We were on the way to the cinema like my note said. When Hannah suggested it I agreed because I thought it would cheer her up. But when we got up there she announced she was going to her friend's party instead. She just walked off, I couldn't stop her, so I had to take her there or she would have gone off on her own."

LIE.

"And you said you'd collect her again at ten, I suppose?"

"I had to," Ellie insisted, "for her own safety, in case she tried to walk home alone. Also, I was worried that Anna's mum would realize she didn't have a lift and call you, and I didn't want to ruin your evening."

Huh! LIE. LIE.

I was just sitting there with my mouth hanging open. It felt like my heart had stopped. How could she betray me like this?

"That's kind of you, love, but you should have called me, never mind our evening," said Dad, more gently. "Why on earth was Hannah dressed like that, anyway? She looked like, well, I don't even want to think about what she looked like."

"Yeah, it was awful," Ellie agreed. "I knew it was a bit over the top, but she begged to try on my clothes, so I let her, to help take her mind off not going to the party. I thought we'd be in the dark cinema by the time she took her coat off and it wouldn't matter."

LIE. LIE. LIE.

Dad would never swallow that lot, surely?

I couldn't believe it when he said, "Don't worry, love. I think Hannah's just trying to be a bit too grown up for her age and getting into a muddle in the process."

"Oh, but I feel terrible," Ellie wailed. "I should have called you the second she walked off to Anna's. I can see that now."

"It's okay," Dad said gently. "You did what you thought was best at the time. None of this is your fault. It's Hannah's mess."

"I'll go and talk to her," Ellie said then. "She must be very upset about letting you down so badly."

"Thanks, love," said Dad, "but I've sent her to bed. Leave it till the morning, okay?"

"Okay," she replied. Then she told him she'd head off to bed herself and they said goodnight. I heard Dad go back into the kitchen and shut the door, and his and Mum's voices murmuring. As Ellie's feet touched the stairs I bolted back into bed and put my head under the duvet.

I heard her creep into my room. "Hannah?" she whispered.

I went rigid and put my hands over my mouth to stop myself from screaming at her. I just wanted her to think I was asleep and go away.

"Hannah, I know you're awake," she said softly. "I'm so sorry tonight went wrong. I should have realized that English suburbia wasn't ready for Paris street style. And I suppose taking the tights off could have just tipped your look in the tarty direction!" She said this with a laugh in her voice, a kind of oh dear, never mind tone that sent a wave of fury rushing through me. "And by the way, I made out to Dad that I didn't know you were planning to go to the party, so let's keep quiet about it being my idea, yeah?"

That's when I snapped. Anger filled me and I sat bolt upright, facing her. "There was nothing wrong with your signal in the cinema, was there?" I hissed. "When you heard my messages and realized our plan had gone wrong you just decided to bail out and leave me to face Dad on my own!"

Ellie laughed. "Chill out, Han! I just forgot to check my phone until about halfway through the film, that's all, and by then I'd got Dad's text too, so I knew there was no point coming to rescue you. And as for fibbing to him, you didn't mind taking the rap for me before, so I thought it would be okay."

"This is different!" I spat. "Surely you can see

that?! Dad's furious with me about tonight, and Mum's too upset to even see me! I thought we'd stand together on this, but you've put all the blame on me! You don't care about me, only yourself! You're a worse friend than Beth. And you're a terrible sister!"

Ellie looked shocked. "How can you say that?!" she gasped. "I'm a great sister! If it wasn't for me, Maya would have gone off with Beth long ago, and the cool girls in your class still wouldn't know you exist, and you'd never have got an invite to that party in the first place... Although, looking back, I guess that might have been a good thing!"

I couldn't believe she was still joking about it! I saw the truth then, and I went shivery and hot and sick and dizzy all at once. I felt like I'd walked into a different universe where everything was turned upside down. Ellie wasn't my new friend, my true friend. "You've just been using me all along, like you've used everyone else," I accused.

"Han—"

"It's true!" I snapped. "You lie to Mum, steal from Dad, get off with Cara's boyfriend behind her back, then use him for money. You just do whatever

158

you want and you don't care about anyone else. Certainly not me!"

"Han, course I care about you!" she protested.

"You **don't!**" I croaked, my voice choking in my throat. "You only care about yourself! You just expect me to keep quiet about you lying and shoplifting and bunking off and smoking, but when **I'm** in trouble you totally abandon me!"

Ellie started saying I was wrong, but I hardly heard her. I was lost in my own thoughts. I saw it then, crystal clear, how she'd walked all over me. I can't believe I lied for her, and smoked just to impress her, and turned a blind eye to her stealing, even when she could have got me **arrested**, even when she took money from **Dad** (of course, I realize now she'd never intended to put that twenty quid back).

Yes, I was angry with her, but I was even angrier with myself. How could I have been so blind? I thought Ellie had turned my life into a fairy tale, but really it's become a nightmare. Then, well, I was so angry, the words just came out. "You don't belong here. I want you to go."

We glared at each other. Neither of us could believe I'd said that.

Then, "You little cow!" she gasped. "How dare you, after all I've done for you?"

I steeled myself, "I want you to go," I said again.

She stared hard at me, and it felt like she was looking right inside my head. "You really mean it, don't you?" she croaked. Then something in her face changed and when she spoke her voice was flat and cold. "Well, newsflash, Hannah, it's not up to you. Sam's my dad too and we want to be together. And FYI, I'm planning to stay even longer than a few months, so get used to it!"

"You can't!" I cried, not caring if Mum and Dad heard now. "Mum's not happy, we can all see that. They row all the time now. You're ruining everything. When I tell her the things you've done—"

Ellie snorted. "And I'll tell her you joined in. What will she think then? Her precious little girl keeping shoplifted stuff, and lying, and smoking. I'll get her up here now, shall I?"

I actually shuddered, just thinking about it. I had to clutch the duvet to stop my hands from shaking. Mum couldn't find out about those things. I couldn't bear it. I didn't think Ellie really would tell, but... I lowered my voice again. "Well, it's only a matter of time before you slip up and she sees what you're really like," I muttered. "Especially without me to cover for you."

"Yeah, well, I'll be more careful from now on, won't I?" Ellie sneered. "I'll just turn on the charm and she'll be onside soon enough."

"She won't fall for it!" I hissed. "Anyway, you're only here as long as I'm happy with it. Mum said so. I don't even *have* to say what you've done. I'll just tell them it's not working out. One word from me and you'll be gone."

"Sam wouldn't let that happen!" she spat, losing her cool. She glared at me. "I'm warning you – you don't want to take me on, sister. You'll lose. I'm here to stay, so you'd better get used to it." She gave me this horrible look, like she hated me. No one's ever looked at me like that before. It made my stomach crunch. Then she stormed out.

Trembling, I turned to my bedside table, and my eyes fixed on the picture frame she'd helped me make.

Those stolen flowers.

Then I looked at the picture itself. Our smiling faces. We looked so happy and close.

All a lie.

I leaped up and grabbed it, pulled out the photo and tore it in two. I shoved the bit with me on in my bedside drawer and I marched across the hall and threw the bit with Ellie on through her doorway. "I don't want this half!" I shouted.

I ran back to my room and slammed my door hard. Then I threw myself onto my bed, flicked off my lamp and cried and cried and cried.

Sunday morning 7.30 a.m.
I've just woken up

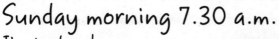

I feel much stronger now. Ellie warned me not to mess with her, but she'll wish she hadn't messed with *me* by the time I've finished! That cow had better start packing, because I'm going straight downstairs now to tell Mum exactly what's been going on, and by the time I've finished Ellie will be on the next train back to Paris.

I just don't BELIEVE this!

When I walked into the kitchen, Dad was sitting at the table with a coffee in front of him and Mum was cleaning out the fridge in her rubber gloves.

"Morning, Hannah," said Dad, looking *not* very pleased to see me.

"You, young lady, have got a *lot* of explaining to

do," Mum snapped. "How *dare* you just go and—"

I cut in. "Mum, please, I need to talk to you. About something way more important than last night."

Well, that didn't go down too well.

Mum did a kind of snort thing and went, "Hannah, this *is* important, and you'd better start taking it seriously, because your behaviour was absolutely disgraceful. How dare you go behind our backs like that!"

"I'm sorry," I cried. "I *am* taking it seriously. But it wasn't just me. It was Ellie's idea, the whole thing. I nearly didn't go but—"

Mum frowned at me. "That's not what she told Dad last night."

"No, it isn't," said Dad sternly.

"You believe *her*, don't you?" I cried.

Dad sighed. "Let's not get into that."

"You do!" I shrieked at him. "You believe her over me! Mum, surely *you* don't—"

"Enough!" Mum snapped. "I'm not even *interested* in who did what to whom. *You* knew it was wrong, Hannah, and *you* still did it."

"I know I did," I admitted, "but Mum, she lies all the time – she told you netball was after school when it was at lunchtime, not that she even went, and she told her teacher she had counselling then bunked off school and—"

Just then the door opened and Ellie burst in. We glared at each other. "I'm telling them everything," I gabbled. "I don't care if I get into trouble too!"

I was sure she'd have a massive go at me in front of them then, and they'd see what she was really like. But instead she just looked upset and confused. "Why would you say things like that, Hannah?" she asked, in a small voice, pulling her hands up into the sleeves of her nightie. "Why are you telling lies about me? I thought we were friends."

Dad looked confused. Mum just stood at the counter, watching us both. "Hannah?" she prompted.

"I'm telling the truth!" I shouted. My mind was whirring, thinking, How can I prove it? I suddenly thought that if I could expose just one of Ellie's lies they'd have to believe me about everything. But what? Then it came to me. "I can prove it," I cried. "She said she didn't get any messages from me last night, but she did. Check her phone." I folded my arms and glared at Ellie.

She made a big show of looking shocked. "I didn't get any messages from you!" she cried. "The first I knew about what had happened was Sam's text. Look if you don't believe me!"

She threw her phone onto the table. As it clattered down I snatched it up, clicked the voicemail icon and scrolled through. I gasped. Nothing there from me. Then I felt so stupid. Of course she'd deleted them! I should have realized she'd have covered her back, she's a master liar after all. I had to think of something else, and quick.

I turned to Dad. "She stole twenty quid from your wallet!"

"Hannah!" Mum cried.

Ellie gasped. "How could you, Hannah? Sam, I promise you, I didn't. I don't understand why she's doing this!"

"Count your money, Dad," I said. "That'll prove it."

Dad shifted awkwardly in his chair. "No, Hannah. If Ellie says she didn't take any money, I believe her."

Ellie gave me a smug look.

ARGH it was SO frustrating I felt like I might

explode. "But she's lying again!" I insisted. "She took it yesterday, just before we went into town."

"Calm down, Hannah," Dad bellowed.

"Sam, maybe you should just check," said Mum quietly.

We all looked at her, surprised.

"You don't believe me!" Ellie wailed.

"It's not that," said Mum. "It's just best that we sort this out beyond all doubt."

"Fine," snapped Ellie, but she didn't look like it was fine. Gotcha, I thought.

You could have cut the tension in the room with a knife as Dad pulled out his wallet and added up what he'd had yesterday morning, plus what he took out from a cash machine last night, minus the taxis.

I felt dizzy with relief. Any minute now they'd see the evidence for themselves, they'd believe me, and Ellie would be sent packing.

I caught her eye and gave her a triumphant smile.

But – "It's all here," said Dad, giving me the most awful look.

I really thought I might be sick then. "What? But how...?"

"I'm sorry I did that, love," he said to Ellie. "I didn't have any doubt about you, not at all." Then he and Mum started having a debate about whether he should have checked or not.

Ellie sneaked a look at me and smirked. "Bank of Jed," she mouthed.

Damn! She must have cadged some money off him at the cinema, and then used it to replace what she took from Dad's wallet while everyone was in bed. Covering her tracks again, after what happened between us last night. I felt like she was two steps ahead of me, like I couldn't think fast enough. I knew I was digging a big hole for myself with Mum and Dad, too. Then it got even worse. Ellie sneered at me and mouthed, "Watch this."

She put a stricken look on her face and started crying, just like that. "She's – she's turned on me," she sobbed. "After things went wrong for her at the party, she just flipped. And now it's like she hates me!"

I couldn't believe it. What an actress!

"Alright, love, calm down, it's okay," Dad said gently.

Mum looked furious now. "Hannah," she

snapped. "I don't know why you girls have had a falling out, but you can't just make false accusations. . ."

WHAT?!

"But I'm not!" I cried. "She did take Dad's money! And she shoplifts. You know those silk flowers on our photo frames? She put them in my bag and I took them without knowing it! I could have been arrested!"

Ellie made herself look as shocked and confused as Mum and Dad.

"Hannah!" Mum cried.

"That's enough!" Dad bellowed.

"Why are you doing this to me?" Ellie whined. "I've only ever been nice to you. I helped you make that photo frame, and redo your room, and I took you and your friends into town. Why do you hate me so much?"

"Because you're a lying, scheming cow!" I yelled.

"YOU'RE the liar!" Ellie screamed back.

"Girls!" Dad shouted, looking horrified.

"I didn't nick anything, Sam," Ellie wailed. "I can find the receipt if you want."

"Ellie, please don't," Dad began, but she marched

into the hall, grabbed her bag from the banister and started rummaging inside, sobbing hysterically.

Dad sighed and rubbed his face, then went after her.

I turned to Mum. "She won't find it," I said triumphantly. "She can't, because if she did, you'd see that those flowers weren't on it."

I stormed into the hall and Mum followed. Ellie was curled up in a ball, rocking back and forth, all her things strewn around her. Dad gave Mum a panicked glance. "I can't find it, I can't, I can't," Ellie sobbed.

"See?" I cried. "How convenient!"

I thought Mum would apologize for doubting me, but instead she gave me a look so cold it took my breath away. "Hannah, go to your room," she ordered. Then she crouched down on the floor beside Ellie and held her tight. Dad put an arm round them both.

I didn't move. "But——"

"Now!" she shouted.

As I stormed up the stairs, Ellie was wailing, "I just want my mum! I want my mum!"

"I know," Mum murmured. "I know."

And for all Ellie's lies and play-acting, I knew she meant that. She does care about someone other than herself. One person: Celeste.

For a moment I really did feel sorry for her. But then I thought of her performance in the kitchen just now and got too angry to care. After a few minutes, Mum came up and told me to go and apologize to her. I didn't want to, but I could see that I wasn't going to get anywhere with Mum and Dad while they were so angry. So I went downstairs, and found Ellie and Dad still standing in the hall.

"Sorry," I mumbled.

"That's okay," Ellie muttered.

"Now shake hands," said Dad, like we were five years old. I didn't want to, but I forced myself to put my hand out. She took it and squeezed so hard it made me wince.

"Can I go and listen to my iPod?" Ellie asked Mum.

"Yes, of course, love," Mum said. Excuse me — love? "And Hannah, we want you in there right now, please." She gestured towards the kitchen door. "We need to have a serious talk."

As soon as Mum and Dad had gone back into the

kitchen, Ellie gave me the most evil look. "I told you not to mess with me!" she hissed. "I told you to keep your mouth shut, but instead you walked right in there and grassed on me. Not that they believed you. Tut, tut, Hannah. Now I'm going to have to make sure they don't believe anything you say about me, aren't I? I'm going to have to make you look really bad."

"Oh, get lost," I managed to stutter, but she'd really freaked me out. It's probably all talk. I mean, it's not like she's actually going to do some terrible thing to me, is it? Is it?

Then she stomped up the stairs and, still feeling trembly, I went into the kitchen.

And I thought that was all bad enough, but the talk I had to have with Mum and Dad afterwards was about the most cringeworthy ten minutes of my life. I thought they were going to go crazy at me. After all, they think I made all that stuff about Ellie up. But instead Mum just took my hand and said gently, "I knew it wouldn't be this easy, Hannah, you accepting Ellie just like that. It's natural to have all kinds of negative feelings about the situation. It's just taken them a little time to surface."

I was staring at her, thinking, What?!

"But that doesn't mean we condone the way you've behaved," said Dad firmly. "Ellie has come here because she needs our help, and however mixed up you feel about it, you can't just tell lies about her."

I was so frustrated, I felt like screaming, except that crying so much had taken all the breath out of me. "But it's not my negative feelings," I insisted. "She did do those things." I gazed into Mum's face, willing her to believe me. Then I said, "I want her to go back to Paris."

Mum gave Dad a look, the kind that said, I told you so, and for a moment I really thought she believed me; that she'd seen through Ellie and would send her back and everything would be okay. But—

"Hannah, sweetheart, just because your dad has another daughter, doesn't mean he loves you any less," she said softly.

"No, course I don't," said Dad, looking bewildered.

"But it's not—" I began, but Mum cut me off.

"I knew these kinds of feelings would surface in the end," she said, giving me a gentle smile. She was acting like I had some kind of emotional problem with Ellie coming! It wasn't about that, though. I was fine with Ellie being here – till I finally realized what she's really like. Mum doesn't understand the real problem – just as much as Dad doesn't. Then she turned to him and said, "I know you wanted us all to slot into place so you could have your perfect situation, Sam, but I'm afraid real life isn't as simple as that."

"Don't patronize me, Charlotte," Dad snapped. "I'm well aware that Hannah has feelings, but there's a limit. After all poor Ellie's been through, too!"

I looked to Mum for support, but she was shaking her head at Dad and sighing loudly.

I felt like telling them that Ellie had just threatened me in the hall, right then. But I knew from what had just happened that there was no point. Mum would think I was making a mountain out of a molehill, because of my emotional problems, and Dad would think I was being unkind to Ellie when she needed us. If I want them to see what Ellie's really like, I'll need hard evidence. So, although it killed me to do it, I made myself stay silent.

"If you have difficult feelings about Ellie, come

and talk to us, okay?" Mum was saying. "We're always here for you, Hannah."

"Okay," I forced myself to say. "Sorry," I added, almost choking on the word.

"Right then," said Dad, clapping his hands together and acting all jolly, "let's put all this silliness behind us and try to have a nice day."

That's when I remembered that we'd planned on going into London to get Ellie's uniform, and look round the shops.

Mum tutted and rolled her eyes. "Typical man!" she muttered. "Just try and sweep it all under the carpet!"

"We have discussed it," Dad said firmly, "and now we're moving on."

So, can you believe it – we're all still going out together! And I have to act like everything's fine in front of Mum and Dad – at least until I can find a way of showing them what Ellie's really like!

Sunday night – what a rubbish day!

Ellie's like two different people since we had the

row. She's all over Dad, and she's started sucking up to Mum as well, to keep her onside. Like, when we went into John Lewis to get her some school clothes she said how all the skirts were so nice she could hardly choose. But then when Mum wasn't looking she did that thing of sticking her fingers down her throat, like they were all so gross it made her sick.

And in private, she's treating me like dirt. We were in this cafe and when I went into the loo she came in behind me and stood at the sink, smudging on more of her dark-blue eyeliner. It was the first time we'd been alone together since it all blew up this morning. I tried to just wash my hands really quickly, without looking at her, but when I glanced up to find the soap squirter she caught my eye in the mirror and said, "See, Hannah? I'm winning already. Your own mum took my side this morning."

"It wasn't like that," I mumbled.

"You're such an idiot," she sneered. "Didn't you think I'd cover my tracks? I'm here to stay, Hannah, whatever you think. And you're not even putting up a fight. It's not even hard."

"You can act as tough as you like, Ellie, and lie all you like," I said, trying to keep the tremor out of my

176

voice, "but I heard you crying for your mummy. That was real."

"Don't you talk about her!" she hissed. "From now on, don't talk to me at all, unless they're listening."

"Fine by me!" I snorted.

"In front of them, you act nice, like everything's fine. And you do what I tell you from now on, or there'll be trouble. Got it?"

"Drop dead," I snapped.

"You will fall into line," she snarled. "Wait and see."

She flounced out and I leaned on the sink and breathed again. My heart was hammering so hard I could feel it in my throat. I tried to tell myself it's just empty threats – but I'm scared. It's horrible, waiting for her to make her next move. I had to force myself to walk out of there calmly, but my legs were trembling as I wiped my wet hands on my jeans.

I was careful to sit next to Dad after that, so that Ellie couldn't, but then she outmanoeuvred me by making a big deal of being beside Mum. She pulled out the bangles she'd bought in Claire's and insisted Mum tried them on, and when Mum ordered a mango smoothie, Ellie did too, saying how yummy it sounded. What hurt most was how pleased Mum looked. Everything inside me wanted to scream, "Can't you see what she's doing? She doesn't really care about you. She's just trying to keep you sweet so you'll fall for her lies." But I made myself stay silent, because I knew I'd just end up looking stupid and jealous.

I ended up looking that way anyway, cos in Topshop Dad was going to treat me and Ellie to these sparkly tops she'd made a fuss over, but I said I didn't want one (no way do I want anything that's the same as *hers*). I tried to do a big smile, to prove I wasn't being sulky and ungrateful, but that just made me feel like crying.

In the car on the way back, Dad and Ellie were singing along to the radio but I just clamped my teeth together and stared out of the window. Mum was shy at first and wouldn't sing either, but once Ellie persuaded her that she sounded fine, she joined in and I could tell she was enjoying herself. It was awful, seeing Ellie twist Mum round her little finger like that, but I knew from this morning there's no point me saying anything about it. I'd just be digging a bigger hole for myself and Ellie would *love* that.

When we got home, I didn't want to stay downstairs with those three so I said I felt like reading and came up here to my room. But I couldn't concentrate on my book. I've got that edge-of-the-cliff feeling again, like the ground's crumbling away under my feet, and my head's all fuzzy and dizzy. I just don't know what to do with myself. Mum thinks I'm the one with the problem, and Dad's angry with me for not accepting Ellie. And I can't trust Maya and Beth after they let me down at the party. I'm completely on my own now.

Monday
Urgh! That was the worst day at school I've ever had

Me and you-know-who left for school together as usual, but as soon as we'd got round the corner I crossed over the road and stormed off so I didn't have to speak to her. She isn't speaking to me either (except when Mum and Dad are around), which suits me fine.

When I went in to registration, this kind of ripple ran through all the different groups of kids sitting on the desks and I knew they'd been talking about me. Jecca did a giggling snort thing and clamped her hand over her mouth, and my stomach turned over. Beth was sitting at her desk next to Maya, copying her Maths homework, and neither of them looked up. I tried to pretend to myself it was because Maths was first thing so Beth had to get it done quickly or she'd be in trouble, but deep down I knew that wasn't the reason.

I sat down in my place beside Maya and got my Maths out too. I did it the night it was set, but I made a show of checking through it again, so I didn't have to look at anyone. I wish you could shut your ears like you can shut your eyes, because I couldn't help hearing Nadia call out, "Nice bra, Hannah! Now you just need something to put in it!"

Jecca cracked up and everyone was looking at me by then. I went bright red and stared at my Maths book. Beth and Maya stayed silent, their heads bent together over their books. Thank goodness Mrs. Jenson came in then, cos I was about to rush to the loos and burst into tears.

Maya did try to speak to me in the cloakrooms at breaktime, but Beth came up behind her and said some horrible things which I can't bring myself to write down in her actual words. It was stuff about how I'm a loser who totally showed them up at the party, and how Maya had better steer clear of me unless she wants everyone to think she's one too. I was getting my apple out of my lunchbox, so I just carried on rummaging in my bag, pretending I hadn't heard. "Are you okay?" Maya asked again, but when I still didn't say anything, she let herself be pulled away by Beth. This is exactly what Beth's been waiting for, a chance to take her away.

My stomach was churning all day and my legs were really shaky. I felt like everyone was whispering about me and laughing behind my back. At lunchtime I sat and read my book (well, pretended to). I picked the bench outside the staffroom, away from the main playground, hoping no one would spot me, and luckily they didn't. I was on edge all day, looking out for Ellie, but I didn't see her, thank goodness. She was probably hanging round the back of the lunch hall smoking instead. If she was even in school, that is. If they hadn't bunked off down the market.

Later on, in Science, Maya and Beth had to talk to me, though, cos we are halfway through doing this forces project together. Because of Mr. Lawler being there no one could be horrible to me about the party, except that when he was writing on the board Nadia got two of the tennis balls we were using for planets and put them up to her chest and smirked at me. I knew she was doing another bra joke, so I just glanced away and stared hard at my books. Maya tutted, but Beth giggled – she tried to turn it into a cough, but I heard it. She was really pally with Nadia and Jecca after that, swapping coloured pencils with them and lending them her scissors and stuff. Maya wasn't sucking up to them like she was, but she wasn't *not* either, if you see what I mean.

When I got in tonight (not with Ellie, luckily – she had "netball" again), I couldn't keep everything inside any more. The second I sat down at the kitchen table I burst into tears. I told Mum all about how awful it had been, except that I didn't mention Nadia's bra comments or what Beth had said to me. I felt too ashamed and besides, the last thing I need is Mum marching down to the school and reporting them for bullying me, when it wasn't really like that. That would just make things even worse than they are already.

When I'd finished talking and managed to calm down enough to gulp some orange juice, Mum said, "It'll all blow over in time. But perhaps you should do something to help things along. How about a cinema trip with Maya and Beth tomorrow after school? I'll meet you all at the gate and take you."

I wasn't sure, but before I could say anything, Mum was calling Sita and arranging it. Then Maya sent me a text to say Beth could come too – I bet she didn't actually *want* to, but of course she didn't want me to do something with Maya on my own, either. Part of me wanted to tell Mum to forget it, after how they'd acted today, but on the other hand they're the only friends I've got, and I'm not exactly going to find any new ones, am I? Not now the entire *year* knows what happened at the party.

So I'm trying to look forward to it. It'll take my mind off my nightmare life, and it'll be nice for me and Mum to spend a bit of time together without evil Ellie there (who, of course, was doing her nice act to Mum and Dad at tea, and when we were all watching TV). Mum's given me the ten pounds for my ticket and popcorn already. That way I can pay for my own stuff like Beth and Maya do, so I won't look babyish having her pay for me. I've put the money in my sparkly silver handbag (it's weeny, so it'll fit in my schoolbag). I've also put in some lipgloss and Starbursts and a travel packet of tissues with pink hearts on. I've hung it on the hatstand by the front door, so I'm all ready to go.

This was such good thinking by Mum. Maybe she's right, and this trip out will win Beth round and we'll all be mates again. Even not-quite-mates like we were before would do.

Tuesday evening
Well, I didn't think things could get any worse but they have

Ellie was waiting for us by the gate.

"Hi Hannah!" she called, and made a big show of hugging me, even though I turned my face away and went rigid in her arms. She hugged Maya too and then Beth, which made them both absolutely beam.

"Why are you still here?" I demanded. "Get lost!"

I was hoping that if I was rude to her, she'd get annoyed and drop her act, and then the others would see what she was really like. But she just smiled even more sweetly and said, "I gave Charlotte a call at lunchtime, to ask if she needed me to pick up anything from the shop on my way home. She works so hard, your mum, I try to help where I can. Anyway, when she mentioned you were off to the cinema I persuaded her to let me take you instead. I thought it would be fun to spend some time with you girls."

I scowled at her, but she nudged my arm as if we were playing a game. "Oh come on, Hannah, there's no need to be in a grump with *me* because your party plan went wrong," she cajoled, like she was just teasing me.

"But it was *your* plan," I cried. "You came up with it! And you even put that outfit together."

Ellie pretended to be shocked. "Don't be such a fibber, little sis!" she cried, as if it was all a joke. "If I'd known what you were wearing I would never have let you out of the house. But I only saw you in your coat."

I turned to Maya. "Surely *you* believe me?" I demanded. But she just looked at Beth and Beth sniggered.

Ellie rolled her eyes and did a big tut. "Oh come on, Han, Maya knows I would never suggest such a slapperish outfit!"

"Yeah," said Beth, "don't be a pants on fire, Hannah. Ellie always looks amazing, she's totally stylish. No way would she have come up with *that*!"

I looked at Maya again, but she was staring through me, weighing up Beth's words, probably deciding that they made sense. Ellie whirled round, linked arms with Maya and Beth and set off down the road. I tried to shout after her but the words caught in my throat.

Maya kept looking over her shoulder at me, and after a few moments Ellie turned and called to me, "Come on, Han, let's not argue. I'm not upset about what you just said to me. I know you didn't really mean it. Let's get going, huh?" And then she set off again, with her new school shirt billowing out behind her in the wind and all her bracelets jangling. Maya and Beth scuttled along beside her, like maids.

I felt like screaming. But I didn't. There were too many people around. People who already think I'm a bit weird, after the party. So instead I clenched my fists and swallowed my rage.

Then I stomped off after them.

I was angry with myself for doing what Ellie expected me to do and following, but I didn't want to go home either. I didn't want her hanging out with my mates without me. Who knew what she might tell them.

But looking back, I probably should have just stormed off right then, because I ended up going home soon after anyway. When we were in the queue for our tickets I reached into my schoolbag and pulled out my silver spangly handbag. I unzipped it and felt for the tenner Mum had given me.

But it wasn't there.

The lipgloss was, and the Starbursts, and the pink-heart tissues, but not the money. I felt around again, then took everything out, held the empty handbag up and peered inside, as if that might make the money magically appear. Some hope.

"Something wrong, Hannah?" Ellie asked.

I glanced up and was just about to explain when I saw the look on her face. I knew straight away that she'd taken my money. "That ten pounds Mum gave me," I stuttered. "It's not here."

"Oh no!" Ellie gasped. "You must have left it on the kitchen counter or something."

I stared straight at her. I should have guessed she'd do something like this. "No I didn't," I said flatly. "I put it in here."

She didn't even flinch. "Well, maybe it fell out into your school bag," she said. "You'd better check."

So, even though I knew there was no point checking, we all left the queue and Maya, Beth and

189

Ellie watched as I crouched down and emptied my bag out onto the scratchy blue carpet. Of course, the money wasn't there.

"It must have fallen out at home," Ellie said. "And we've only got a few minutes before the film starts. I don't have any spare cash."

"I've only got enough for my ticket and popcorn," said Beth.

"Me too," said Maya. "But how about if we put our popcorn money together, would that be enough to get Han a ticket?"

Ellie shook her head, looking regretful. "Tickets are seven quid, so it wouldn't be."

Beth looked relieved. She clearly hadn't wanted to give up her popcorn money so I could get in.

"In that case, maybe none of us should go," Maya suggested. "We could do something else instead."

I felt like hugging her.

But then a horrible thought struck me. If we did something else, say, they came back to ours, or if we all went into town, Ellie might find another way of showing me up. The safest place for her was in a dark cinema where she had to be silent. Plus, Beth was looking really annoyed. She'd been on about seeing *Fame Academy: The Movie* for ages. If she missed it because of me she'd be even more determined to shut me out for good and just make a two with Maya.

My stomach lurched as I realized that the best thing was for them to go in without me. I felt like throwing up, but I made myself smile. "I think you guys should see the film," I forced myself to say. "I'll be fine. I'm not too bothered about it, and I don't want you to miss out."

"Great!" said Beth, grinning.

"Are you sure?" asked Maya. I couldn't meet her gaze. I knew that if I did I'd start crying. So I looked at the floor and nodded.

And that was the worst thing of all. That "Are you sure?" was all Maya said. I mean, we've been best friends for years and I only got one single "Are you sure?"

"Well, if you insist, Hannah," Ellie said breezily. "You can always see it when it comes out on DVD, anyway."

"It's fine," I mumbled. "Have fun." It nearly choked me to say it, but I had to keep up my act.

As they joined the queue again, I headed for the

doors. I didn't want to give Ellie any more of a victory, so I made myself walk slowly and calmly, when what I really wanted to do was bolt straight out. But as soon as I was outside and round the corner I ran as fast as I could, heart thumping in my chest, tears pouring down my face, all the way home.

When I got in I tried to dash straight up to my room, but Mum heard me and came into the hallway and I ended up sobbing in her arms. She sat me down at the kitchen table and was just making me a hot blackcurrant when the door clunked again and Dad came in. He looked surprised to see me, and a bit annoyed – Mum must have told him that she'd be home after all, because he'd obviously come back from work early so that he could talk to her on her own. When I saw him I burst into tears again, and soon I was sitting between them, telling them what had happened at the cinema, how my money had vanished and how I knew exactly who'd taken it.

"I don't believe this," Dad muttered, rubbing his face. He gave me a look of total exhaustion. "I thought we'd put this kind of thing behind us."

"Hannah, if you're making this up—" Mum began.

"I'm not!" I insisted. "Look, nothing else had fallen out of my handbag, the money wasn't in my school bag and it's not anywhere here." I gestured round the kitchen.

"It probably fell out in the hallway somewhere," said Dad, only just managing to stop himself from shouting at me. "Have another look."

I almost dissolved with frustration. "She's really nasty to me when you're not around!" I cried. "And now she's stolen my money and ruined my chances of making up with Maya and Beth!" I turned to Mum. "That's why she offered to take us to the cinema, not as a favour to you. She's only being nice to you so you don't send her back."

"Hannah, sweetheart, you're just getting yourself all worked up now," said Mum gently. "I'm sorry you're finding things difficult with Ellie at the moment, but you can't make serious accusations without proof. Why don't you go upstairs and have a quiet think about things. Then we can talk about this again when you've calmed down."

"I am calm!" I screamed. "You want proof, I'll give you proof!"

Suddenly I found myself marching to the door.

I pushed a chair out of my way, and it toppled over and crashed to the floor behind me. I stormed across the hall up to the hatstand and began riffling through the pockets of all the coats and jackets, then turning the sleeves inside out, and even unfurling all the umbrellas and frantically shaking them. I needed to prove that the ten pounds wasn't there. Then they'd *have* to believe me.

By the time Mum came out I knew it wasn't in any of the coats or umbrellas and I was halfway through tipping all the shoes and boots upside down and banging them on the tiles. I was still sobbing like mad, hurling things on to the floor instead of putting them back properly. "It's not here!" I cried. "See?"

Mum just stood there in silence, with her arms folded. Dad appeared in the doorway behind her. "I told you!" I yelled. "It's not—"

But then the worst possible thing happened.

As I picked up one of Mum's ankle boots, a crumpled tenner fluttered out.

I stared at it in disbelief. Then my heart caught in my throat as I realized – Ellie was one step ahead of me again. Of course she hadn't just *taken* the money, full stop. She'd snuck it out of my purse and made it look like I'd dropped it, so that no one would believe my story.

I was so swamped with frustration I couldn't even speak. I just staggered up the stairs and into my room. I could hear Mum and Dad following me, but I wedged my door shut with a pile of rolled-up mags. Dad rattled the handle for a while and Mum kept saying, "Please unblock the door, darling", but I stayed silent, curled up on the rug. Finally Mum said, "Let's just give her some time, Sam."

As they walked away I heard Dad say, "I thought we'd raised Hannah to be more generous than this."

That cut right through me. Why couldn't he *see*?

"Give her a break," Mum snapped. "This isn't easy for her."

"Oh, you're *loving* this, aren't you?" Dad countered, his voice raised, exasperated. "You're so pleased that there's a problem! You haven't even tried to make this work!"

I heard Mum's sharp intake of breath. "How dare you, after all I've done for *your* daughter," she gasped, then went pounding down the stairs.

Dad swore loudly, then called out, "Look,

Charlotte, I didn't mean it like that," as he followed her down.

I don't know what else they said after that, but they've been arguing ever since. I can still hear their muffled voices in the kitchen. If this goes on, maybe they really will end up getting divorced.

I can't take it any more. I have to do something. If I don't act now, I'll always be looking over my shoulder, a nervous wreck, waiting for Ellie to make her next move.

The second she walks in that door I'm going down there to have it out with her, once and for all. Somehow I'll make her slip up and show her true colours in front of Mum and Dad.

Tuesday still

Mum's just called tea, but I've said I don't feel well and I'm going to bed. I don't want to see any of them right now, especially not Ellie. She's just – it's – I don't even know what to say any more.

When she came in I stormed downstairs. The kitchen door was just swinging shut behind her and

I was about to burst straight in but I made myself stop and listen. The door didn't quite close and I could just see Ellie. I couldn't *believe* what she was saying to Mum and Dad. The blatant lies she was telling. She said she'd suggested we all do something else when I couldn't find my money, but that Maya and Beth had insisted on seeing the film. She said, "Hannah didn't seem to mind. She told us she'd run home, get her money and ask Charlotte to drop her back at the cinema. I tried her mobile but she wasn't answering. We waited ages for her, but we had to go in in the end, because we'd already paid for our tickets. But we didn't really enjoy the film, we were too busy worrying about her. Is she okay?"

"Yes, she's fine, love, she's upstairs," said Dad. *Love*. The word made me wince.

"But why didn't she come back?" Ellie asked.

I was amazed by her nerve. *She* didn't know what I'd told them. *She* didn't know how they'd reacted. And yet she seemed absolutely certain that either I hadn't said anything or that, if I had, they hadn't believed me.

"She thought you'd—" Dad began.

But Mum cut him off. "She made a mistake about

something, that's all, and she got a bit upset. I have to go and get the washing in now." Then I heard her walk off through the utility room.

"So what's up with Hannah?" Ellie asked Dad.

"Nothing for you to worry about, love," he said wearily. "She's just, er, having a hard time adjusting to you being here. But you must never think it's anything you've done, okay?"

Ellie's eyes widened and she made a big show of looking concerned. "Is that why she said all that stuff about me the other day?"

Dad nodded. "It seems so. But you mustn't worry about it. Things will settle down in time."

ARGH! Enough was enough. I began opening the door. But then Ellie said something that made me freeze.

"Okay, Dad."

Dad? I felt like I couldn't breathe.

"Dad?" said Dad.

Ellie looked startled herself. "Oh, sorry, I just... I mean, is it okay if I call you that?"

"Of course!" he told her. "It's wonderful."

I quickly pulled the door to again, before Dad saw me. I wanted to bolt back upstairs, but I forced myself to stay put, listening.

"I thought me and Hannah were getting on well," Ellie was saying in a hurt, bewildered voice. "I've tried really hard with her, and with Charlotte too, even though I know she doesn't want me here."

"Of course she does," Dad insisted. "It's just taking her a bit of time to get used to things, that's all. And Hannah, too. But don't worry. They can both see how lovely you are. Things will work out in time."

"Oh, Dad, I really hope so," Ellie said. "I love being here with you."

"I love you being here too," said Dad, his voice thick with emotion.

Neither of them spoke for a while, then Ellie said, "I've been thinking... Maybe, if it's okay, I'd like to stay till the end of Year 11 and go in for my GCSEs. I didn't think I'd have a chance of getting decent grades, not after what happened at school in Paris, but I'm working hard and catching up now."

The sneaky little so-and-so! She did mean it when she said about staying longer. That's over a year! And what about afterwards – A-levels? Uni? I bet I know why she wasn't on track for any qualifications in Paris. She probably got expelled for bad behaviour!

"I'm so glad you're enjoying school here," said Dad, "and I'm really proud of you for working so hard."

At that point I had to clamp my hand over my mouth so I didn't splutter and give myself away. Working hard? As if! She wasn't even in lessons half the time and the only homework she ever gave in was the stuff I'd done for her. Once again I could have kicked myself for falling under her spell.

"There would be a lot to sort out, and we'd have to really think it through," Dad was saying then. "There's your mum to consider."

Ellie made herself look tragic. "I can't go back, Dad, I just can't." She made her voice sound urgent, desperate, like she was really scared of leaving here. She's such a good actress and she's got him wrapped around her little finger.

"I understand, love," he said. "I want you to have the same chances other kids your age have. And this might be the best place to get them. I'll talk to Charlotte about it, when the time's right. If she agrees, we'll see what your mum thinks, when she's a bit better."

Huh? What about talking to me as well? He's

obviously forgotten all that stuff about taking this one day at a time and Ellie only staying if I'm happy. Or maybe that was just nonsense he came out with to make me feel involved.

Ellie flung her arms around his neck and said, "Thanks, Dad," like it was all decided.

"I'm so proud of you, love," Dad said.

"And I'm so glad you're my dad," said Ellie.

I felt like storming in there and shouting, actually, he's MY dad and you'd better stay away from him! But instead I heard her chair scraping back, and I bolted upstairs before she came out and found me. I crouched behind my closed bedroom door and waited for my heart to stop pounding.

That's when I realized what I have to do.

I get it now.

Just marching in and having it out with Ellie won't work. She's too clever for that. And I'll never be able to show Mum and Dad what she's really like because she covers her back so carefully. And even if I did find something, some evidence, well, I'm sure she'd wriggle out of it somehow. If I want to beat her, I have to be stronger, and smarter, and tougher. I have to play her at her own game. Okay, so maybe my life wasn't perfect before she came, but at least it was mine.

And I want it back.

Yes, I'm scared. I admit it, she scares me. I know what she's capable of. I mean, Mum and Dad and Maya and Beth probably all think I'm a spiteful, jealous little liar, thanks to her. But I also know that if I don't do something to stop this, she could wreck everything.

I can hardly believe I'm even thinking what I'm thinking. But I'm desperate. I need to get Ellie back to Paris and out of our lives. NOW. The only person who really matters to her is her mum. That's her only weakness. I don't feel good about dragging Celeste into this, but I don't have any choice.

Wednesday after school

Dad came home early again and he'd obviously been talking to Mum, because when I got in they were both sitting at the kitchen table with empty coffee cups in front of them. They were doing this fake jolly thing like we were in a TV sitcom, with Mum fussing round getting me OJ and cookies and Dad announcing that he'd booked a court and we were all going to play tennis in half an hour. It was so obvious they'd come up with that to try and get me and Ellie back on track. Of course I said I didn't want to play, but Dad just did a big fake laugh and clapped me on the shoulder. "It's about time for the first game of the year, Han," he said, acting all matey. "Let's see if your old dad can still beat you, eh?"

When Ellie got in and heard about the tennis plan, she didn't want to go either. But of course, she's still pretending to be the perfect daughter, so she couldn't complain that much and when Dad jollied her along she had to go upstairs and get into some shorts. And naturally, she used it as another chance to get Mum onside. When we started to play, she really laid it on thick, sucking up to her by saying she was improving all the time, even though she kept hitting the net. And she was playing the little girl with Dad again, getting him to help her with her backhand. Then when they won, she rushed into his arms and gave him a massive hug. As he lifted her off the ground, I breathed in sharply – I felt squeezed in half, as though my stomach was being wrung out like a dishcloth.

Of course, as soon as Mum and Dad went into the sports club to get us all some drinks, she turned on me. "Okay, sister," she snarled. "One on one. Out of three. May the best girl win."

I gave her a dirty look and took my place. I didn't even want to play at first but once we got started, something inside me just took over. She blasted a serve at me, obviously expecting me to miss, but I lunged for it and smacked it back expertly. It skimmed the net and bounced at the baseline, just in, and I won my first point. It was total no-holds-barred war after that. I've never played with such focus in my life. I threw myself at her ground strokes and blasted them back with topspin. Our volleys were fast and furious. If there hadn't been other people on the courts, I think we probably would have ignored the ball and just hit each other with the rackets instead. We won one set each, and neither of us was backing down.

But then I saw my chance to put my plan into action. Every bone in my body was willing me to win that final game, but I knew that to win, to really win, I had to lose. I let a couple of shots go through, and pretended to be massively annoyed about it.

Ellie was jubilant. "Ha! You managed to hold me off for a while there, but now I'm getting the better of you," she crowed. I gave her another dirty look and waited for her to serve for the final point. I hit the ball back a couple of times, so as not to be too obvious. And then, when she smacked it hard at me, I didn't dive out of the way and prepare to strike back. Instead I let it go slamming into my leg.

"Ow!" I screeched. I didn't have to fake that – it really stung.

For a moment I felt bad about what I was about

to do. Her mum's still in hospital, after all. But the look of satisfaction on Ellie's face when the ball hit me – well, she had to go. I limped up to the net.

"You've won," I said, and held out my hand.

Ellie looked at it, a triumphant smile on her face. I didn't just mean the tennis, and she knew it.

"Look," I continued, "I won't try to fight you any more, or say anything else to Mum and Dad about you. I'll do whatever you tell me to. But please stop being so nasty to me. Please, Ellie."

Ellie stared hard at me, and I tried to look as pathetic as possible. Then she smiled her wicked smile, and shook my hand. "About time," she said. "You can start by carrying my bag for me, and tonight you can do my Maths homework."

"Okay, Ellie," I stuttered.

And with that she strode into the sports club. I trailed after her, struggling under two bags, still wincing and limping, but inside I was coiled up, wired, like a snake, ready to make my next move. I'm still like that now. It's a horrible feeling, but I have to go through with this. I need her to think I've given up, so she doesn't suspect anything.

So then tonight, after tea, Ellie came into my

room without knocking to take my hairdryer (which she's now decided is *her* hairdryer and I have to ask if I want to borrow it). As I handed it over, I said, "Oh, the phone rang while you were in the shower. Dad answered. I think he was talking to your mum." I made myself say it slowly, casually, even though my heart was pounding in my throat. Just for a moment, something flashed across her face – fear, worry, panic? – I don't know, but I could see I'd thrown her off guard. I did feel guilty, but then I thought about the way she'd used me, all the lies she'd told about me, and I held my nerve.

"It can't have been," she said. "She would have asked to speak to *me*, and Dad didn't say anything when I went downstairs just now."

"Oh, okay. I must have made a mistake," I said. "You're right – she'd definitely have asked for you – after all, she hasn't ever rung before."

"She hasn't been *able* to," Ellie snapped. "She hasn't been well enough. The doctors said so. I'm in contact with them every few days. They would have told me if there was any change."

I shrugged. "Yeah. Of course. It can't have been her. I must have got it wrong. Sorry, I shouldn't have mentioned it." I walked over to my desk and started setting out her Maths homework with my back to her. Then I casually added, "I just thought maybe it was her because Dad was saying how well you'd settled in, and how she mustn't worry because he'd look after you for as long as necessary."

I flicked through her Maths textbook, letting it sink in. Letting her realize that it must have been Celeste.

"But what did he say? When's she coming out of hospital? When can I see her?" she demanded. "I'll go and ask Dad now—"

"Don't!" I cried, seeing how my plan could all unravel in front of me. I had to hook her in – and fast. "Look, Ellie, I'm sorry," I said, more gently. "I wasn't going to tell you this. I did hear everything they said. It was her. It sounded like she was begging for you to visit, but Dad said you were doing just fine here and that you didn't need the upset of seeing her. He told her not to call again, at least not for a while."

Ellie looked stricken for a moment, and I nearly cracked and confessed that I'd made it all up. But then her face hardened again. "Maybe he's right," she said. "He's only trying to protect me after all. And I don't want to go back, anyway. I like being here with my dad."

That stung me like a slap in the face, but at least it helped me to push my guilty feelings aside and carry on. "Of course," I said. "But you must want to see your mum. Just for a visit. Just to check she's okay. I know if it was my mum in hospital, I wouldn't want her to think – well…" I let the unspoken words hang in the air.

"Think what?" Ellie demanded.

"Well, that I didn't care about her," I said. "But I'm sure your mum doesn't think that," I added quickly.

"I'm desperate to see her," she mumbled, more to herself than me. "I know Dad thinks it's a bad idea, though, and I don't want to upset him. Not when it's so obvious I'm his favourite."

I wanted to yell at her for saying that, but I kept my head. This was my chance. Ellie had a dilemma and she needed a solution. And, of course, I came up with one. I didn't worry too much about the guilty voice in my head – it had quietened down a lot when she'd said she was Dad's favourite.

"We could go and visit your mum, make sure she's okay, make sure she knows you're thinking of her," I said quietly.

"But how, without going against Dad's wishes?" Ellie demanded.

I tried to look like I was just working it out there and then. "Dad doesn't need to know," I said slowly, pretending to think on the spot. "We could go to school as normal, then get the train into town and take the Eurostar from St. Pancras. You could visit your mum and be back by teatime. We could make an excuse for being late home, say netball practice for you and, I don't know, art club for me."

For a moment she looked excited, then her face fell. "But the doctors said I shouldn't visit her for a while," she mumbled. "They said she needed some more time to recover first."

"I bet they only said that because Dad told them to," I countered.

But she was still uncertain.

"Of course, do whatever you think is best," I made myself say, trying to sound casual, like I didn't mind either way.

"But she'll think I don't—" Ellie's voice cracked

and she trailed off. Then she took a deep breath, and came right up close to me. "Why are you helping me?" she asked, narrowing her eyes suspiciously.

My heart was hammering so hard in my chest I was worried she might hear it. "I just thought... If it was my mum..." I began, feeling my mouth go dry. She had to believe me, or my whole plan would be ruined.

Ellie stared hard at me for a moment. Then her gaze softened. "Okay, we'll go," she said. "I don't have any money so you'll have to get my ticket sorted."

"I've got sixty-three pounds saved up in my piggy bank," I told her. "That should cover it."

Ellie snorted. "As if! It's, like, about a hundred and fifty quid each or something. You'll have to borrow Dad's credit card and book online."

My heart started hammering even harder. I had no idea the tickets were so much. What on earth have I got myself into? If Dad finds out, he'll kill me. But hopefully, with the other trips he's made on the Eurostar recently, he won't look too closely at his statement. Or if he does notice maybe he'll think it was one of those online fraudsters. There's no way

I'm pulling out now, though. This could be my only chance to get rid of her. "Alright," I said.

"We'll go on Friday," she told me. "You've got tomorrow to get it sorted."

"Okay, Ellie," I said meekly. As she stalked out, I turned to my desk, my heart hammering. I feel like the lowest person on earth for bringing her mum into it, but at least it's done. Everything's fallen into place.

Hopefully, when Ellie sees how happy Celeste is to see her, and they realize how much they've missed each other, it'll be enough to make Ellie want to go back there, but I have to be there too, just in case it's not. I might have to get Celeste alone and insist that Ellie goes back. If I need to, I'll tell her that Ellie's miserable here and cries herself to sleep every night but that Dad's really strict and mean and she's too scared to tell anyone how she feels in case he gets angry with her. I'll tell her he's been angry with her before, *very* angry. I'll say that if she can't go home yet, Ellie would still be better off in foster care nearby for a while than at ours, so at least that way she can visit every day. I'll tell her anything – anything to make her insist that Ellie goes back to Paris.

Right, time to "borrow" Dad's credit card and get online. I can't believe I'm about to do any of this, but then, desperate times call for desperate measures, as they say. Anything to get this half a sister out of my life for good.

Thursday, very late

Well, I've done it.

I got the train times to London from here off the web last night at the same time as I was booking the tickets for Paris. I checked the information carefully, to see what we have to take. As well as our passports, we need a letter from Dad giving us permission to travel alone. Then I logged on to Dad's hotmail account and within a few minutes there was a confirmation e-mail from Eurostar with our e-tickets attached. I printed them out then deleted the mail and deleted it again from the deleted items folder. After that I went down to the hall and slipped Dad's credit card back into his wallet, then came up here to my room to write the fake letter from him. I just hope I get away with this, I really do. I couldn't bear for him to find out what I've done.

Ellie was in bed when I crept in to her room a

few moments ago. She was plugged into her iPod again, and she only took out one of the earphones to listen to me. "Well?" she snapped.

"We'll set out for school as usual," I whispered, so as not to wake Mum and Dad, "only we'll need to get going by 7.30, cos it'll take us half an hour to walk all the way up to the station. We need to get the 8.08 train at the latest, to give us plenty of time to go through security and get onto the Eurostar. It goes at 9.26. I've written the letter we need from Dad authorizing us to travel alone." I stared through her as I said all this. We hadn't spoken all day, apart from politely and stiffly in front of Mum and Dad, and she'd ignored me the whole way home as usual. "We arrive in Paris at 12.47 p.m., allowing for the hour's time difference," I told her. "And we can get a cab to the hospital."

"You'd better bring your savings for that," Ellie whispered. "I need to keep my money for drinks and stuff."

I felt like yelling at her, but I bit my lip and carried on. "We'll have to be back on the 3.13 train that gets into St. Pancras at 4.36, so we can be home at 5.30 at the latest. That gives you almost two hours with

Celeste. Tomorrow morning when I tell Mum I'm staying late for art club, you should say you're doing netball, and that we can walk back together. That way she won't turn up to get me. Okay?"

"I suppose," she said.

"And don't forget your passport," I added.

"Like I would," she sneered. Then she put the earphone in again and turned her back to me. And that was it. Sorted. We're really doing this.

Friday
I'm quickly writing this while Ellie goes to the buffet car

We're on our way.

We got here just before nine and we had to walk through the station to get to the escalators that take you up to the Eurostar bit. Walking round with Ellie, I kept expecting people to stare at us, to wonder what we were up to, and why we weren't at school. But no one did. They were all too busy bustling up escalators, steering their wheely suitcases round other people with wheely suitcases, and browsing in the shops.

Anyway, as soon as we got on the train at St. Albans Ellie had nipped in to the loo and put on her blue-turquoise chiffon dress-top thing and some purple tights, and lots more dark-blue eyeliner, and her stripy glovy-sleevy things. She looked at least sixteen, and maybe not like she even still went to school. I wish I'd thought to bring something else to wear. I feel like an idiot in my uniform.

The man at passport control barely looked at us, security was fine, and no one wanted to see my letter. And beeping the barcodes on our tickets at the entry gates was easy.

Ellie's being less snotty to me too – she really believes I've given up fighting her. She even said thank you when I got us drinks and sandwiches just now. I usually have a packed lunch anyway, but with everything I had on my mind this morning I ended up leaving it on the side. Oh, she's coming back, gotta go.

Saturday morning, back at home

It feels like a million things have happened since I last wrote in here. Yesterday was a long, long day. You won't *believe* what—

But, hang on, I'll start where I left off, so I don't miss anything out.

Okay, so, where was I? Ellie and I were on the Eurostar, eating our sandwiches from the buffet car.

And then my phone rang.

Without thinking I just picked it up. But the name on the display stopped me dead. It was Dad. My mind went into overdrive. "He must be on to us or why would he call?" I stammered. "But how did he find out? He'll be so worried. I'd better—"

But Ellie lunged across the table and grabbed my arm. "Please don't answer, Hannah," she begged. In her panic she seemed to forget to just *tell* me what to do, like she usually does. "We'll explain later.

He said outright that he doesn't think I should see Mum yet. And he'll be furious about his credit card. He'll probably make us turn round and go straight home. Please, let's just go and visit her, and then we'll call him back. Promise."

I was torn. It made me feel sick, thinking that Dad didn't know where we were. Had he called Mum at work? Were they out looking for me? Had they realised that Ellie had gone too? I pushed those thoughts out of my mind. This was my one chance to get rid of her and get my life back, and I had to take it. I was doing it for them too, for all of us. I bit my lip and turned off my phone. Then I shoved it right down into the bottom of my bag, so I didn't have to look at it.

After that we finished our sandwiches, avoiding each other's eye, and then Ellie spent the rest of the journey hidden behind a *Grazia* she'd bought at the station. I'd brought my book but my mind was racing too much to read, so I just stared out of the window. I'd felt so in control, like as long as I planned everything down to the finest detail, Mum and Dad would never find out. And now the plan was ruined and we weren't even in Paris yet.

But it was too late to turn back.

When we got out at the Gare du Nord, Ellie led the way to the taxi rank, and explained to our driver in French where we were going. The journey took about fifteen minutes, and I stared out of the window, but I didn't take anything in. As we slowed down opposite the tall metal gates of the hospital, the driver indicated, waiting for a gap in the traffic to turn into the gravel driveway. But Ellie said something to him, handed over some of the Euro notes she'd got at St. Pancras (with my savings), and leaped out of the cab, pulling me with her. The cabbie drove on as soon as she slammed the door, and we had to wait ages for a break in the traffic before we could cross the busy road. I remember wondering why she didn't want him to pull in properly, but I soon found out.

The hospital was a big white building that looked more like a stately home. We walked up the path along the side of the driveway and I headed for the front entrance. As I went up the steps, I could see a reception desk inside, with a woman on duty, a coffee machine, a couple of leather sofas and a palm plant. I was about to step inside when Ellie grabbed my arm and pulled me back down. "What are you doing?" she hissed.

I was confused. "Well, how else are we going to see your mum?" I asked.

"We can't just walk in, you idiot," she whispered. "They'll want us to sign a form and show some ID. They'll find out who I am, and that I'm not 18. Then they'll ask where Dad is and when we can't explain they'll try to ring him and everything'll be spoiled. Mum's told me all about these places."

I was thinking, *What places – hospitals?* but I didn't say it. Ellie was frustrated enough with me already. "Well how are we going to get in then?" I asked instead.

Ellie sighed and flicked her long dark hair back over her shoulders. She looked around, lips pursed. Then she spotted an old wooden gate held half open by a wheelbarrow full of hedge trimmings. "We go through there and get in round the back way," she said, like it was obvious.

"But we can't, that's—" I began.

Ellie gave me a look. I knew what the look meant. I'd stolen my dad's credit card, bunked off school and was now in Paris when I should have been in double English. What was a little sneaking around compared to that?

I reminded myself of why I'd done all this. This was it. My chance to get rid of her. And I wasn't about to miss it, not for anything.

So we slipped through the gate (we had to go right past the gardener's back — luckily he was listening to his iPod). Then we hurried along the path on the other side, keeping a look out. Ellie ushered me up to a window and we both peered inside. What I saw surprised me. Instead of rows of beds and people in plaster casts and stuff, there were tables and chairs, and a TV. Two women were playing chess and someone was doing a puzzle. No one was wearing pyjamas.

"She's not there," said Ellie. "I suppose she might be in the garden."

"The garden?" I repeated. "I didn't know hospitals had gardens."

But Ellie just grabbed my hand and pulled me into a little alcove, out of sight. We glued ourselves to the wall, holding our breath, as a nurse walked past. Then Ellie was running down the path, fast, streaking along, and I was struggling to keep up with her. The path led through a little archway and opened out onto a wide sweeping lawn. I dashed past beds of pink and purple flowers, and a fountain. There were a few spindly metal tables with matching chairs scattered around. It looked more like a hotel than anything else.

Then Ellie saw Celeste, sitting at one of the tables, and she ran so fast she stumbled and almost tripped over. As she neared her, though, she stopped still, and let me catch up. "Keep watch for me," she said, panting for breath.

Then Ellie walked towards her mother. Celeste looked up and gasped. As Ellie got closer, she stared at her, with a strange wide-eyed look, as if she couldn't quite believe what she was seeing. I could definitely tell she was the same woman as in the picture Dad has, though her black hair is cut into a harsh bob now, and her face is thinner and kind of sucked in. But she was still beautiful, her eyes still bright and bewitching, like Ellie's.

Celeste reached out a hand and as Ellie bent to hug her she stroked her hair in wonder. "Oh, my baby," she murmured. "My baby, my girl. You've come, at last. They said you wouldn't, but I knew you would. I knew it. My angel."

Ellie couldn't say anything. Tears were running down her face.

"I'll get out of here," said Celeste. "Today. Right now. We'll go home. I'm never going to let you go again."

Then she was crying too and Ellie was howling and sobbing, and they were holding each other so tight it seemed like they'd never let go.

Whatever I thought of Ellie, I couldn't help but be moved too.

And, as for my plan, this was perfect. I was just doing the best thing for everyone – getting Ellie out of our lives and back where she belonged. Okay, so Celeste had a plaster cast on her leg, and some kind of strapping on her wrists, and there were crutches propped against the table, but apart from that she looked fine. The hospital must have just been over-cautious, keeping her in, or maybe it was because she couldn't manage on her own at home. But she wouldn't *be* on her own now – she'd have Ellie. I was thrilled – perhaps things would work out even better than I'd hoped. Maybe Ellie could just go home with Celeste today, without the *need* for some sort of temporary foster care.

For a moment I really thought I'd done it.

But then everything changed.

It was like a cloud coming over her face. Celeste's, I mean. It happened when she held Ellie away from her, by the shoulders, as if to look at her properly. Her smile went in, like the sun, and then she was shaking Ellie hard, and screaming in her face. "Get away from me," she spat, still clutching her tight. "You put me in here, you bitch! I hate you! I should never have trusted you. You planned this all along – with them. My own daughter – the shame! I never want to see you again. Nurse! Get her out of here! Nurse!"

And then someone was running over, calling out for others to come and help.

For a moment I was just staring, gaping, but suddenly I found my feet. I dashed over and prised Celeste's fingers from Ellie's shoulders. I grabbed Ellie's hand and pulled her away. She kept looking back at her mum, a kind of stunned horror on her face. "What on earth just happened?" I gasped, as I pulled her along, across the lawn. A nurse was coming through the archway, so we dashed straight ahead onto a patio and then through some doors into a conservatory. I headed for the only place I could think of, and luckily I knew the French for it, so I could follow the signs. I held tight to Ellie's hand and she ran with me, stumbling, in a daze, all the way to the ladies' loo.

It was only when we were safely locked in the disabled cubicle that I realized how shaken up I was too. But I hardly had time to register that, because Ellie was absolutely hysterical. I tried to sit her down on the closed seat of the loo, but she leaped up again. "Mum's right," she muttered to herself, still gasping for breath. "It's my fault she's in here. I called the ambulance."

I still didn't understand. Looking back, I can't believe how stupid I was being. "But that's good, isn't it?" I asked. "You needed help."

But Ellie hardly seemed to hear me. I finally got her to sit down and handed her some loo roll for her nose, but she just stared at it, like she didn't even know what it was. "It's my fault," she said again.

"Of course it's not," I insisted. "She didn't mean those things she said. The accident must have traumatized her. She's not thinking straight. I've seen it on *Casualty*."

"Oh, typical of you to pussyfoot around, Hannah!" she wailed. "You *know* what's wrong with her!"

I just looked at her, completely confused. Then Ellie was looking at *me* blankly too. "Oh my God. Dad didn't tell you, did he?" she said.

"Tell me what?" I stuttered.

She sighed deeply. "The crash. It wasn't an accident. Not exactly. She's... She's not well. She's not been well for a long time. She gets paranoid sometimes. You know, she worries, like, *obsesses* over stuff, and gets all confused and frightened. The doctors are saying she's schizophrenic. That night, she thought some people were following us, in the car behind. Government people. She said they were watching the apartment and we had to get out, that's why we'd got in the car in the first place. I knew they weren't, of course, but I couldn't let her drive off on her own. I knew there wasn't *ever* anyone watching us, or stealing our post, or tapping our phones. And that night I tried to tell her no one was following us, again and again, but she wouldn't believe me. She kept spotting different cars and saying they were all part of it. We drove for hours. This voice in her head was saying they were out to get us, because we had some secret information, and she was listening to it and not to me. She put her foot down to get away and even when it was just us on this little road, she wouldn't slow down. The car just got faster and faster and then..." She winced at the memory.

For a moment I was completely stunned.

It wasn't just Celeste's bones that were shattered, it was her mind too.

Ellie was shivering, huddled up, with snot and tears still running down her face. I just stared at her, with no idea what to say. This stuff didn't really happen to normal people, in normal life, did it?

I felt sick with myself for what I'd done. I was way out of my depth. Blind panic rose up in my chest and I tried to fight it down. Ellie was still talking.

"I blacked out for a moment. Then when I came round I saw...we'd crashed into a massive tree. Mum was really still, sobbing. I could see her leg was broken. And her chest, she'd hit the steering wheel and — there was so much blood. Her clothes were soaked in it." She clamped her hand over her mouth, almost wretching at the memory. "I managed to get the door open and go round to her side. I didn't want to move her, but there was smoke coming out of the engine and I thought the car was about to blow up. She screamed in agony as I pulled her out onto the grass." She shuddered, as though she was hearing that scream again.

"Oh my God," I murmured.

"I didn't know how to stop the blood. Then she started having trouble breathing and she lost consciousness and I just couldn't wake her. It was late at night and we were out of the city by then, in the middle of nowhere – there was no one to help us. That's when I crawled back into the car and found my phone and called an ambulance. I didn't know where we were, but I remembered the name of this little place we'd just come through, so they managed to find us and took us to hospital and soon after, the questions started. Why did we crash? What had she been doing, driving so fast? I ended up telling them everything. The woman was really nice, and I was still in shock...it was good to have someone to talk to. I thought that was all it was, a chat, but really they were trying to find out about Mum. How could I have been so stupid?

"So, when she was stable and had recovered enough, they did their own psychological assessment and transferred her here. Maybe they wouldn't have even thought to do that if I'd kept my mouth shut. I should have taken her home as soon as the plaster was on her leg and wrists, and her ribs were strapped up. I should have put her in a wheelchair and sneaked her out. Then she wouldn't be in this place. It's my fault she's in here."

"It's not," I said gently.

I fell back against the door with surprise as Ellie suddenly leaped up. "It is!" she screamed, kicking the bin hard. It smashed into the wall and fell over, spilling out paper towels and other rubbish. "It's my fault she's in here and now she hates me!" She kicked the bin again, denting the metal, and again, and again. It crashed and rolled around the cubicle, like it was trying to get away from her.

Suddenly the door to the ladies' swung open. I lunged over and grabbed Ellie, clamping my hand over her mouth. We both stood still, trembling, trying to control our breathing. Whoever it was opened each of the cubicle doors one by one, then finally went into one. I reached over and flushed the loo, trying to make things sound normal. Then I ran the tap. After a moment the other loo flushed and the main door swung open and shut again – thank goodness. Maybe it was someone looking for us, or perhaps they were just finding the cleanest of the loos, I don't know.

I let Ellie go and she slid down the wall and began to sob hard. I was absolutely shaking then, my heart hammering. I didn't know what to do. I wanted to go and find someone to help, but I'd believed what Ellie had said about us getting into serious trouble if we made ourselves known. "Ellie, I'm so sorry," I told her. "Coming here was my idea. This is all my fault."

"It's okay," she sniffed, staring straight ahead. "You were only trying to help."

I took a deep breath and tried to calm down. The whole thing had gone way out of control. However hard it was going to be, I knew I had to confess.

It was time for the truth.

"No, I wasn't," I admitted. "I wanted to get rid of you. I thought if you saw your mum you'd realize how much you missed her and insist on coming back to Paris straight away. So I pretended she'd rung. But I had no idea what was really wrong with her. I just thought you'd both been in a crash. I don't know why Dad didn't tell me that there was more to it. If I'd known the whole story I'd never have put you through this, whatever I thought of you. Never."

I braced myself, waiting for Ellie to shout at me, but instead she just stared. "You had a plan all along?" she asked. "I'm impressed. I never would have guessed it. I thought you were way too timid to fight back." She raised a wobbly smile.

"Well, yeah, I did — but I swear to you, I didn't mean for this to happen," I said again. "I honestly didn't know about your mum."

Ellie shrugged. "It's okay. Well, it's not, but… you know. I thought you knew but were too freaked out to mention it. People are. I knew I couldn't cope with her myself any more. I felt terrible about leaving her, but I didn't know what else to do."

She paused, uncertain, and I nodded for her to go on. "Mum had talked about my father a bit over the years, but I'd never been bothered about finding him. I figured, if he didn't want me, I didn't want him. I had no idea she hadn't even *told* him about me. Then when this all happened I thought, why shouldn't he look after me? I just wanted someone to look after *me* for a change."

"So you tracked Dad down?"

"Yeah." Ellie suddenly burst into tears again. "I abandoned her, Hannah. I just left her in this prison and tried to start a new life. How could I do that? To my own mother?"

"Come on, what else could you do?" I said gently. "It's good that she's in here. They're helping her. And you couldn't live on your own, could you?"

"I suppose not," she choked out, still sobbing hard. "But still, maybe I should have just stayed in that foster home, then at least I could have seen her every day."

"But she hasn't been well enough for visits," I said softly. "You saw that for yourself."

"Perhaps. But I should have been here, nearby, just in case. I'm an awful person, Hannah. And you must have been desperate to get rid of me, to do all this. I've been terrible to you too, haven't I?" She sighed deeply, then she said, "You must hate me for the way I've treated you."

"No, not hate," I said automatically.

Ellie looked at me and raised an eyebrow.

"Okay, a bit hate," I admitted.

"I can't believe how I've acted," she mumbled,

looking at the floor. "I suppose, well, it's just that I felt all twisted inside, all sick and scared, and I kept thinking what Mum must think of me for getting her locked up in this place. It didn't seem like a big deal at the time, doing bad stuff, and getting you to cover for me. But I can see now that I shouldn't have got you involved."

"It was my fault too," I admitted. "I should have stood up for myself more."

She shrugged. "Maybe. But then when you did, after the party, I was even *worse*. I should never have left you to take all the blame in the first place and I shouldn't have been so mean to you after we had that row. I was just so scared of being sent back here, of having to cope on my own again. And I couldn't believe you'd even said that, about wanting me to go – especially because I thought you knew about my mum." With that, she burst into fresh sobs.

"Oh, Ellie, I'm so sorry I ever said I'd get you sent back," I stammered, choking up too. "I realize now how panicked you must have felt. You'd just found somewhere safe to be and I threatened to take it away from you. If only I'd known about your mum, I—"

Ellie cut in. "No, it's my fault. You're right, I did

panic, I was just so scared. I know it was awful, but I thought if I made you scared too, by being mean to you, you'd keep quiet about wanting me gone. And I thought I had to make Dad and Charlotte think that you were the one with the problem."

I smiled grimly. "Well, it worked."

Ellie smiled a little too. "Not completely. I really believed you'd given in after the tennis, but you were still fighting, you had your own plan. You're stronger than I thought."

I sighed. "Maybe. But you really scared me, Ellie. I thought you didn't care about any of us. I thought you were going to ruin our lives."

She looked so upset then. "Han, I'm so, so sorry," she said, staring straight into my eyes. "I'm not really like that, I promise. And I do care, about all of you. I'll put things right with Dad and Charlotte. I'll tell them everything if you want me to. I just… Everything spiralled out of control. Can you ever forgive me?"

I shrugged. The truth was, I wanted to forgive her, but I didn't know how, not after everything she'd done. She'd hurt me so much, I didn't know where to begin.

"Well, I just hope you'll give me the chance to prove how sorry I am," she said then. "That's all I'm asking for, Han, a chance to try and make it up to you."

"Mmm," I said, cos I didn't know what else to say. I stood up and pulled a bit of tissue paper off my knee. "Urgh," I groaned. "I don't even want to think about where that's been." That made her do a grossed-out face too, and a wobbly smile.

Then I found myself rummaging through my bag.

The phone in my hand felt like my own magic wand. I clutched it tightly as I slid down next to Ellie and pressed green. It beeped and lit up and I scrolled through a ream of missed calls, maybe ten or twelve. All from Dad.

Ellie was staring warily at it, as if it was an unexploded bomb. "Please, Han, don't ring him," she begged.

"He'll know what to do," I reasoned.

"But we can think of a plan ourselves, work out a way round this," Ellie gabbled. "Maybe he doesn't know I've gone as well. Maybe we can still get back in time and you can make something up about why you weren't at school. I could come home as usual.

We might get away with it." She was desperately trying to find the right thing to say, the thing that would make me put the phone down. When I didn't she got really, really anxious. "If he finds out what we've done, he'll be furious," she wailed. "I knew he didn't think it was a good idea for me to see Mum yet, and I went behind his back. He'll hate me after this. He won't want me any more. Mum's much worse than I imagined – even I can see she's not fit to come home. And anyway, even if she does get better, she'll never want me back. She hates me."

I wanted to say, *No, she doesn't*, and *Everything'll be fine*, in that automatic way you do when someone's upset. But I just couldn't see how it would be, so I didn't say anything and it felt really awkward.

"When Dad chucks me out I'll never see you again," she said then. She paused, staring deep into my eyes in that way she has, as if she was looking right inside my head. "And I feel like I've only just seen the real you."

That was when, for the first time, I saw the real Ellie too. I saw her as just a teenager instead of almost an adult. I saw how scared she was, and I knew how scared I would be too, in her shoes.

But I had more faith in Dad than she did.

"It's not true about Dad," I told her. "He'd never give you up. And he'd never give up on you. We're his girls. He loves us and he'll always love us, whatever we do."

I'd never thought that until right then, when it came out of my mouth. But as soon as I said it I knew it was true.

Ellie sighed and pushed her hair back from her sticky, wet face. She didn't look like she completely believed me, but she looked like she wanted to. "Okay," she said. "Call him."

At first Dad was just relieved to hear my voice, but then he got angry, saying that Mum had dropped my packed lunch into school during registration and when one of the secretaries called up to my form room for me to come and get it, they'd found that I wasn't there. Then he said (well, shouted) that they were both out of their minds with worry and what the hell was I playing at? But as soon as I blurted out where we were and what had happened he went very calm and businesslike. He just said, "Okay, don't panic. Look after Ellie, get yourselves something to eat, and I'll be there as soon as I can. I'm leaving the office right now. Tell Ellie not to worry about Celeste. When I get there we'll go and talk to the doctors properly, together."

"Okay, thanks, Dad," I managed to mumble. It was such a relief, I nearly started crying myself.

When I told Ellie what Dad had said, she calmed down a lot, but she still didn't want to go and sign in at the desk, or let anyone know we were there. "Let's go back to my apartment," she said. "We've got loads of time, and I'd like to collect a few things."

I thought that was a good idea. I didn't fancy waiting for hours in the disabled cubicle of a ladies' loo. Ellie still wouldn't go up to the desk, so we had to sneak back out the way we'd come in. This time it took ages for the gardener to move far enough from the gate for us to slip through unnoticed. I thought we'd need to get another cab, but Ellie said she knew the way and we both felt like a walk.

We wandered back down the main road and headed further into the city, through narrow streets full of cafes and boutiques. Sleek black cars glided past us as we walked down wide boulevards lined with grand white houses. I felt as if my eyes had opened for the first time all day. It was a beautiful spring afternoon in Paris, with pink blossom fluttering from the trees like confetti. The smells of the city were all around us, too – petrol and perfume, cigarettes and coffee and bread. A chattering family spilled out of a doorway right in front of us, and a glamorous woman passed us, her tiny little dog in a diamanté collar trotting behind her. The pavements were packed with cafe tables and waiters in black brought teeny espressos and giant lattes out to customers basking in the sunshine.

We walked on and on, through main streets and side alleys – Ellie seemed to know the city backwards. We turned into a scruffier neighbourhood, with boarded-up shopfronts covered in torn posters, graffiti sprayed on the walls and music blasting from some of the windows. I'd never been anywhere like that before and I stuck close to Ellie.

Soon we entered the courtyard of a grand old building. It was beautiful, but kind of crumbly at the edges, and it desperately needed a fresh coat of paint. Washing was hanging across between the broken iron balconies. There were some old car seats set among the weeds in the courtyard, as makeshift benches. As we neared the main door, a jagged chorus of barking started up.

"*Bienvenue*," said Ellie, with a grin. She was trying to hide it, but I could tell she was nervous about going back to her apartment. We'd climbed up to the fourth floor, past radio noise and cooking smells. I noticed her hands shaking as she fumbled for her keys. She paused for a moment and breathed in sharply before opening the door.

Ellie told me it looked exactly the same as it had the night everything happened. A social worker had brought her back the next morning, to collect a few things, and then again when she was meeting Dad, but no one had been there since.

The first thing that hit me was a damp kind of smell, like towels that haven't dried out properly, and something else, perhaps a bin that needed emptying, or a blocked drain. We'd come straight into the front room and, when I looked out at the balcony, I saw the sari curtains Celeste had made. They were really beautiful. I said so and Ellie gave me a small smile. An old brown sofa with the stuffing coming out of one arm took up most of the space and there were French film posters on the walls, stuck up with Blu-tac. On a blocky wooden coffee table, covered in an Indian sequined cloth, sat a stack of tatty magazines and a few cups that had mould growing on the dregs inside.

As we stared into them, Ellie said, "When they brought me back to pack, to come to yours, the social workers realized that no friends or neighbours had been in to clean up," she explained. "They did want to send someone in to do it, but I made excuses, kept the keys, said I'd post them. I didn't want them touching our stuff – I knew the cleaning was just an excuse, and that they'd clear out our things and give our apartment to someone else. They chased for a few days, but luckily they stopped after that. Then, I guess, we must have got lost in the system."

"Or maybe they did just want to do the cleaning," I suggested. Ellie gave me a puzzled look. "Huh! Yeah, maybe they did," she said, obviously amazed by the thought.

After that I didn't know what to say. I couldn't even imagine living in a place as gloomy and run-down as that apartment, but, to Ellie, it was home.

"I'll just grab some stuff from my room, won't be

a sec," she said as she vanished through a curtained doorway.

"Okay." I wandered into the tiny kitchen area and idly slid open a drawer. It was full of teaspoons – as in completely full, as in there were about 200. I was a bit startled. No one could need that many teaspoons, could they? I opened a cupboard and closed it again quickly – the bread inside it had gone completely green. There were newspaper clippings stuck to the fridge with magnets. They were in both French and English, and I noticed that they had scribbly writing all over them. They seemed to be about government business, and some of the names were underlined. In between them were post-it notes with indecipherable scribbles on and arrows pointing to the clippings. I walked back into the living room, shuddering. The stuff on the fridge had freaked me out a bit, and besides, the gross smell of the rotten food in the kitchen bin was making me want to throw up.

I stood by the balcony for a while, but ages later Ellie still hadn't come out, so I went to find her. Her room was like a magic grotto, with fairy lights and fabric wall hangings strung everywhere. The floor, chair and dressing table were covered in dirty clothes, magazines and make-up. Ellie was sitting on her bed, staring into space, hugging a toy rabbit. He looked a bit like my Jasper.

I sat down beside her, but I didn't say anything. Instead I just stroked the rabbit's ears.

"Eduardo. He's my favourite," Ellie said after a while. "I've had him since I was two."

"Why did you leave him behind?" I asked.

Ellie hugged Eduardo tighter, as if to show him that she hadn't left him, well, not really, not for ever. "I knew I was going to my dad's," she said. "I knew he had another daughter. I was worried you'd think I was a baby for turning up with a toy rabbit."

I laughed in surprise. "I actually put Jasper, my rabbit, on your bed to welcome you," I explained. "But then I nipped in and took him back, cos I was worried you'd think I was a baby!"

Ellie laughed. "Really? That's spooky!"

And then she started talking, really talking. Some of the things she told me made me want to cry, like how her mum often forgot about practical things and so sometimes, when she was little, she went out to play with dirty clothes and greasy hair and got teased. And when Celeste was following some kind of cult spiritual teaching where she hardly ate, she wanted Ellie to do it as well, and got angry that she wouldn't join in.

But there were the lovely things too, things that made me smile, like when they used to bake fairy cakes and have candlelit picnics on Ellie's bed and tell stories and make up funny songs. And when they lived in Spain and started feeding the stray dogs until they had a pack of about eight who followed them around, and Ellie would spend whole days playing with them.

"Things started to get more difficult when we moved here," she explained. "I'd always just thought our life was normal, even with all the ups and downs. But when I started school here I realized how different Mum was to everyone else's parents, and I began to question some of the things she believed in. And I wished I could do what the other kids did, like go on school trips. But there was no way she'd have let me go away overnight. Some days it was hard enough to persuade her to let me leave the apartment long enough to go to school."

"Sounds great! Mum never lets me have a day

off!" I said, then cringed. "Sorry, that was a stupid thing to say," I mumbled.

"No, Han, it's fine," Ellie promised. "I want you to act normal around me, not walk on eggshells."

"Okay," I said, feeling embarrassed all the same. "So, tell me what else happened."

Ellie sighed. "She started acting more strangely, or maybe it was just that it freaked me out more because I was older, and I knew it wasn't normal. She kept saying people were spying on her, watching her. One day it was the government, the next it was the man from the *tabac*. She wanted the curtains shut all the time, so we compromised with the saris. At least they let some light in. I got more and more worried about her and tried to be with her all the time. I started missing school, and my friends drifted away. I can't blame them, I mean, I stopped hanging round with them in the evenings and never invited them back here. So you see, I really did understand your fears about Maya and Beth, and honestly, I really did want to help you with the party outfit. It's just, when it all went wrong, I was so scared of being sent back, I thought I had to make Dad think it was your idea."

"Ellie, don't worry about that now," I said gently.

"That's all behind us. Tell me about your mum. Was she always this way?"

She sighed. "Yes, on and off, but it was getting worse. I used to rush home the moment school ended, to check she was okay, but sometimes I was too late. Like, she wouldn't be here, and I'd find her in the park or down by the shops, muttering to herself or confused about where she was. Sometimes she'd go out in the middle of the night, in her slippers, and I'd have to walk the streets trying to find her. She was frightened all the time, and that made me frightened too. I gave up my own life to look after her and it still wasn't enough to make her better."

"I know," I said gently. "But that wasn't your fault. You did the best you could."

"Thanks, Han," she said, managing a small smile. "I don't think I did, but, well, it's good to talk about it." Then she stood up and stretched. "I guess we should get going." She found a bag and gathered up the things she wanted until it was stuffed full. Lastly, she rescued a pair of jeans from under the bed and when they wouldn't fit into the bag she pulled them on over her tights.

As I waited, I gazed into Ellie's mirror, staring at

myself, thinking, *I can't believe I ever worried about inviting Maya and Beth home, just in case Dad cracked a lame joke or Mum asked us to turn the music down.* I felt totally spoiled and pathetic. Compared to Ellie's situation that was nothing. No way could she bring anyone back here. I mean, imagine never knowing how your mum's going to act, or being scared of what you'll find when you walk in the door. Mum's always there when I get home, ready to get me some OJ and hear about my day. Of course, it's not Celeste's fault she's ill, it must be terrible for her, but just thinking about being in Ellie's shoes makes me appreciate my own mum so, so much.

"Okay, I'm ready," said Ellie, pulling a few more bangles and bracelets from the dressing table up onto her wrist.

I felt completely miserable then, thinking how I've taken Mum for granted, and feeling so sad for Ellie. But suddenly my stomach did a really loud rumble and we both looked at it in surprise and we couldn't help giggling, even after such a serious conversation. I hadn't even thought about eating since we were on the train, but I suddenly realized how hungry I was.

"Come on," said Ellie. "Let me show you the best little patisserie in Paris."

She pulled the door shut behind us with a decisive slam and turned the key briskly in the lock. Then she headed down the stairs without looking back.

Saturday still, a bit later on. Everyone's having such a lazy day after yesterday that I've got loads of time to write in here.

So, anyway, to carry on, we got back to the hospital just as a taxi crunched up the gravel driveway. Dad got out and I felt a rush of relief at seeing him.

Ellie was looking nervous, though.

As he strode up to us, I wiped my mouth on my sleeve. I didn't want him to see brioche crumbs and think we were having some kind of jolly day out. Despite what I'd told Ellie even *I* was a bit worried about what he was going to say.

But he didn't say anything at all. Instead he just scooped us into a hug.

Ellie buried her face in his shoulder. "I'm so sorry," she muttered. "Please don't send me away."

"You wouldn't, would you, Dad?" I said. I reached for Ellie's hand and clutched it tight. She clutched mine back. I realized then that I wasn't just asking for her sake. I was asking for mine too. Maybe forgiving Ellie wouldn't be so hard after all.

Dad looked startled. "Of course I wouldn't do that!" he cried. "I love you girls. I'll love you for ever, whatever you do. Anyway, I should be apologizing to you." He held Ellie away from him, by the shoulders, looking pained by her tear-stained face. "I'm so sorry, love, I completely misjudged things. I didn't want you to see your mum, not yet anyway. She needs time to get better, and I was worried something like this would happen if you saw her. I thought it would set you back, and that you needed a decent chance to settle in with us. But I was wrong. I should have known you'd be desperate to see her, whatever her reaction."

Ellie could have blamed me then, said that I'd persuaded her to go, or even worse, told him why we were there, but she didn't, thank goodness. Instead she just said, "It's okay, Dad."

He hugged her tight again. "I'm so sorry you didn't feel you could ask me to bring you. Things will change now, though. We'll talk to each other. Really talk, okay?"

Ellie nodded and burst into tears again against Dad's chest. When Dad gave me a wobbly smile over her head I saw tears in his eyes too.

We went inside and while Dad filled in a form and Ellie washed her face in the loos, I got us hot chocolates out of the machine. None of us said anything as we waited in the reception for a doctor to come and talk to us, but it didn't feel awkward. Actually it was nice in a strange way, just being quiet together.

After a while a tall slim man with a bushy beard came in and introduced himself as Dr. Howard. He explained that they'd had to call him in specially because it happened that none of the doctors on duty that day were fluent in English. He shook Dad's hand and, when Dad introduced me and Ellie, he shook our hands too. Then he led us into a small office, we all sat down and Dad told him about us trying to see Celeste and what had happened.

Dr. Howard sighed and rubbed his balding head. "I wish you girls had come up to the desk," he said. "We could have helped you. Apparently the nurses tried to find you, to see if you were okay." Then he turned to Ellie and said, "Now, perhaps the best thing is for you to ask me any questions, or tell me any worries that you have, anything at all, and I'll do my best to help and to explain the situation with your mum, okay?"

Ellie nodded. Then Dad asked if she'd rather talk to the doctor alone, but she said she wanted him to stay, and me as well. She was silent for ages, while Dr. Howard just rearranged some things on the desk and gave her lots of encouraging smiles. Then she said, so quietly that you could hardly hear her, "She hates me cos it's my fault she's in here."

"You saved her life," said Dr. Howard firmly. "With bleeding as severe as that, and internal trauma – if you hadn't called for help she wouldn't have made it. As for your mother being transferred here, and anything that happened afterwards, well, that has been completely out of your control. Celeste's not the way she is because of anything you've done. It's down to her illness. The schizophrenia. And she doesn't hate you. She was just shocked at seeing you today. From what the nurses tell me, it sounds like she got confused and frightened because of her illness, and that's why she ended up lashing out at you."

"She used to do that at home sometimes too," Ellie admitted. "She'd accuse me of being one of them. But I never knew who she meant. She said she was watching me, that she knew what I was planning, that she was on to me."

Dad and Dr. Howard's faces were carefully neutral, but when Ellie glanced at me I couldn't hide my horror. "Not always," she added quickly. "We had loads of good times too. Sometimes she was fine for months – virtually. And she's really fun and clever and talented. I'm glad she's my mum."

I gave her a wobbly smile, and Dr. Howard said, "It's okay to talk about the hard times, Ellie. You're not betraying your mum by expressing your feelings. We all understand that she behaved the way she did all those times because she is ill. It was out of her control and she certainly wouldn't have meant to hurt your feelings."

Ellie looked suddenly desperate and my own heart lurched in my chest. "I want her to come home," she croaked. "I can look after her, I always have. And I'm older now. And I've got Dad and

Hannah to support me. They can come over to visit all the time and—"

Dr. Howard smiled sadly. "I'm sorry, Ellie," he said. "I'm afraid it's out of the question. She didn't mean to put you in danger in that car, of course, but that's what happened. And we know from our assessments that this is the best place for her, at the moment anyway, so that she can't hurt you or herself. We can help her to get better, to control her condition so it's easier to live with. She'll probably never be cured as such, it doesn't really work like that. But she's here now, and she's made a start. That's the main thing."

Ellie nodded slowly, taking it all in. She didn't look as if she quite believed him. But at least she was listening.

Then he explained what they were doing for Celeste and what had been happening. He said that for the first few days after she was admitted to the hospital she was given heavy doses of antipsychotic medication and spent most of the time sleeping.

He also said they'd given her some medicine to help with the horrible voices that she hears in her head, which make her so frightened. And once her symptoms are under control, she's going to be having psychotherapy. He explained that it will help Celeste to make sense of what's happening to her and express her feelings about it. It will mean lots of talking, but also doing things like art, drama and music.

Ellie seemed pleased. "She'll like that," she told him. "She's brilliant at drawing and she can make things too – with fabric, or wood, or anything you want."

Dr. Howard smiled. "Things should start to get better now," he said. "She's safe here, and the treatment will help her to understand what's happened to her. And most importantly, she's got a good reason to get better."

Ellie looked puzzled. "And what's that?" she asked.

"You, of course," said Dr. Howard.

Ellie gazed at him. Then, for the first time since he'd led us into that office, she smiled.

We had to get a later train back, so Dad sorted out changing our tickets (he even managed not to go nuts at me about his credit card). And he bought us ham and cheese croissants and OJs from one of the stands in the station.

As the train sped on, Ellie started shivering and Dad gave her his sweater. Of course, it was way too big for her, but she curled up in it like a cat and soon she was fast asleep, with her head on my lap.

There was something nagging at the corner of my mind, something I'd wanted to ask Dad, but not in front of Ellie. "Why didn't you just tell me the truth about Celeste in the beginning?" I said softly.

He looked surprised, then sighed and shook his head. "I don't know," he said. "You seemed too young, somehow, to deal with that kind of stuff. I suppose I was trying to protect you. I should just have been honest. You're a lot more grown up than I realized."

I was pleased about that. I didn't say what I was thinking, though, which was that I feel like a different girl from when I first found out that Ellie was coming. Well, perhaps I'm just a different version of the same girl. I feel like I've grown up a lot. Maybe that Hannah couldn't have handled the truth, but this Hannah can.

Dad's voice cut into my thoughts. "I have to be honest with you, love," he said gravely. "Celeste isn't coming out of hospital, well, not for a long while anyway. It's for her own safety, and Ellie's. Of course, Ellie can make her own choice when she's eighteen, about whether to live with Celeste if she's well enough. But, depending on how you and Charlotte feel, and if she still wants to, I'd like her to stay with us till then, at least."

I just stared at him.

"I know this hasn't been easy for you," he gabbled, "and I know we all have a lot to sort out still. And I understand if you don't feel that it's what you want. If you're not happy about it, it won't happen."

I was still silent, staring.

Dad nudged my foot under the table. "So, what do you think?"

"It's cool," I said.

"*Cool*?" he repeated. "Is that it?"

I smiled. "Yeah, Dad, that's it."

He shook his head, and nudged my foot again. I nudged his in return and we started having a foot fight, but then we nearly woke Ellie, so instead Dad checked his messages and I got my phone out too. There was something I needed to do. I thought I'd find it hard, sending Maya that text, but it wasn't, not really. I basically said that I didn't like the way Beth treated me and I wouldn't be hanging round with her any more, so it was up to Maya if she still wanted to or not.

I didn't get a reply.

Typical Maya, avoiding the issue as usual. Whatever she decides in the end, I've had it with Beth. I'm not going to run around trying to make her like me any more. That's all over. I'm the new Hannah now, and the new Hannah only wants *real* friends.

After that I stared out of the window for a long time, in silence, even though there was nothing to see but blackness and our own reflections. Not that I even saw those – I was lost in thought about Ellie's life. I wanted to tell someone about it, to stop it going round and round in my head.

"You should have seen it, Dad, where they were living," I whispered, and he put his phone down on the table. I told him about the awful smell and the weird stuff on the fridge and all the teaspoons. And about Ellie having to look for her mum when she went missing, even in the middle of the night, and not daring to leave her to go to school, and getting teased when she was little about her hair and clothes.

When I finally stopped talking, Dad looked so sad and old and tired that I almost wished I'd kept it to myself. "Oh, I've been so naive," he sighed. "Trying to make everything fine all the time – I suppose I didn't want to think about the damage Celeste's illness did to Ellie, or what it must have been like for her – living with it for all those years, with no help, and moving around all the time. I so badly wanted to believe she was okay that I just swallowed it when she put on that happy act in front of me. Your mum did warn me but…" He sighed, rubbing his face. "Can you believe it, I accused Charlotte of not wanting things to work out, when she was only trying to put Ellie's *real* needs first. She even suggested we arrange some counselling for her, but I shrugged it off."

I felt sorry for Dad, but also glad that he was really talking to me at last, having a proper conversation, instead of just treating me like a little girl.

"I'm so sorry I haven't been understanding enough of your feelings, either, Han," he said. "I tried to gloss over the problems between you two with shopping and tennis because I was desperate for things to work out the way I wanted."

Of course, that was my chance to tell him what Ellie had really been like. But I didn't. That's all over. Instead I just said, "Dad, honestly, we've put our differences behind us. Everything's fine now."

"Thanks, but it isn't," he said firmly. "I'm pretty useless, and now I've got *two* girls to be a rubbish father to."

"You're not a rubbish father," I insisted. "You're brilliant. Well, apart from the corny jokes. And I wish you'd buy some trainers – *no one* wears black lace-ups with jeans."

He grinned then. "Well, maybe you could take me shopping, Miss Style Guru. Can't have me showing you up, can we?"

I could have said that he doesn't show me up, but I didn't. Instead I just stuck my tongue out at him and asked for some money for the buffet car. There's no harm in keeping parents on their toes, is there?

When we got back in to St. Pancras, Mum was there to meet us. I couldn't wait to see her so I rushed off the train first, straight up the platform, through the open luggage gate and into her arms. She hugged me tight, whispering, "Oh, Hannah, I was worried sick," into my hair.

I hugged her back, until she prised me away and looked into my eyes. I realized that she wasn't just worried, she was angry as well. "This was all that girl's doing, wasn't it?" she snapped. "I can't believe she dragged you off on her crazy scheme. Anything could have happened! I'm going to have words with—"

Ellie and Dad were coming up the platform. I shook my head. "No, Mum, it wasn't Ellie," I insisted. "It was *me* who persuaded her to go to Paris. Honestly. The whole thing was my idea."

Mum stared at me as if I was a stranger. She just didn't know what to say to that (she said a *lot* about it this morning when we were in the kitchen together, and I said a *lot* of sorrys, and things are okay between us again now, thank goodness).

Then she spotted Ellie and I could tell she was shocked. Ellie looked so pale and dishevelled and defeated. All her make-up was gone, apart from the smears of mascara smudged down her face, and her eyes were red and raw from crying. Her colourful clothes were hidden under jeans and swamped in Dad's too-big sweater. She walked slowly, shoulders hunched, exhausted.

Suddenly Mum rushed up to her. I thought she was going to go mad at her too, but instead she just wrapped her up in a big hug, and didn't let her go for a very long time. After a moment, Ellie hugged her back, almost collapsing onto her. I felt so proud of Mum and grateful too. I really wanted her to make Ellie feel better.

That was when Dad started blurting out all this stuff to Mum about how sorry he was, and what an idiot he'd been, and how she was right about Ellie's needs, and my feelings, and everything else. She just smiled and put her hand on his arm to stop him. "There's plenty of time to sort all that out later," she said. "Come on. Home."

We didn't talk much on the train back, and we took a taxi from the station instead of walking. When we got in Mum made us all a quick supper of tomato soup and buttery toast. After that she ran Ellie a bath and put her nightie out on the bed for her, like she used to for me when I was little. Then she tucked her in, with Eduardo the rabbit next to her. And she tucked me in too. Of course, Ellie won't let her do that every night, and I won't either, well, not for ever, anyway! But last night, after everything, it felt just right.

Oh, gotta go, Mum's calling me down to help with lunch. I guess no amount of family drama is going to get me out of setting the table. Oh well!

Hey, wow!
I just found this notebook down
the back of my chest of drawers!

I was looking for my light-blue hair clip (no idea where that's got to!) and I found this and ended up having a quick look through, then getting comfy on my bed and reading the whole thing. Three and a... no, hang on, nearly four months have gone by since me and Ellie went to Paris. For a while I meant to keep writing, but things just got so busy, and then I lost this book. I did look for it a few times, but then I forgot all about it. But now I want to write a little bit more, just to finish off the story of me and Ellie, to say how everything ended up.

Well, the answer is, things ended up pretty good. Ellie is here to stay. Celeste's a lot better and Ellie visits her often, with Dad, and even once with Mum. She's still in the hospital at the moment, but the doctors are talking about maybe moving her into a little flat in a sheltered accommodation scheme, when the time is right. But Ellie won't be able to live there too, and it might be years before Celeste's well enough to be completely independent.

Ellie's still very sad about that, of course, but she's doing well here.

Dad began helping her with her Maths and got her a tutor for Science, and once she started doing better at school she stopped bunking off. She wants to go to fashion college now, so she'll need to get good grades. On Wednesday nights she sees this lady called Caroline, who's a counsellor, to talk about her feelings. And she says it does help. She talks to me too, of course. I mean, we *really* talk, a lot, and at nights Mum sometimes has to come out of their bedroom and send me or Ellie back to bed because we're whispering in the dark.

Ellie's going in for her GCSEs (she's chosen Art and Textiles as her options) and she's made even more friends at school. She doesn't hang round with Jed and Cara any more, well, not much, cos they're kind of losers. Her new main friends – Melinda, Alfie and Jakz – are still really cool (of course!) but they actually *go* to lessons. And when they go out they sometimes take me along with them. I've been to the cinema a few times with them and they always buy me sweets and popcorn and stuff. We've been down to the skatepark too, after school (Ellie texts Mum first now!). Nothing ever happened with Tom, by the way. You never know, though – he flipped right off his board the other day while we were watching, and Ellie said he lost it on the half-pipe cos he was trying to show off to *me*! I don't know if he was – but maybe!

Things were tough at school for a while after I broke friends with Beth. I just stopped hanging round with her, right from first break on that Monday, and she soon got the message. I'd hoped Maya might take my side, and I was upset when she didn't, but I know now that true friends are loyal, and if she can't stand up for me to Beth then maybe I'm better off without her. I was really scared about being on my own, but I hung round with Ellie and her mates a bit, and became a library helper on Wednesday lunchtimes, and joined in the French skipping with Rhianna's lot from 8K. So it wasn't too bad, well, not as bad as I'd thought it'd be, anyway.

Then I made friends with this girl called Charlie who started coming to my stables. She's not in my class but we meet up most break and lunchtimes. And we hang round together on Saturdays too, because we stay at the yard all day to help out. We love it and Mum's pleased cos we get our lesson free now in return for all the mucking out and grooming and stuff we do. We sometimes have sleepovers afterwards, round here or at hers, and watch DVDs and eat ice cream (Ellie's special sundaes have become famous in this house!).

I do some extra stuff now too, like playing netball (maybe one day I'll make the school team, like Ellie has), and after school on Thursdays I go to art club.

Things are pretty good at home as well. Sometimes I spend time with just Mum, like going to see a film or getting our nails done or something. And Ellie goes to aerobics with her most weeks, just the two of them. And sometimes I do stuff with just Ellie. We go shopping loads (like she promised, she's never shoplifted again, or stolen from Dad, but she hasn't lost the knack of wrapping him round her little finger for cash!). I don't want to dress exactly the same as her any more, cos I'm not sure her style really suits me (and no, Mum still won't let me wear the short dress with just tights combo!) but she's helped me a lot with finding my own style.

Don't think we have this perfect life now or anything, though – I borrowed Ellie's new silk scarf last week without asking and she had such a go at me! And Mum gets cross with us when we row over who used the last of the nice shampoo and things like that – and then Dad acts like we're all so annoying, going, "Women!" and burying his head in the paper. But anyone can tell he's really happy.

Anyway, I like all the ups and downs. They mean that we're just being ourselves, our real selves. I love it when we go to Burger Nation all together and me and Ellie try to nick each other's chips and Dad tells an awful joke and Mum makes us actually eat the bits of salad, even though I keep telling her they're just for decoration. Times like that are the best. That's when I feel as if I'm standing outside of us and seeing what other people must see.

They'd see a normal family, just like everyone else's.

And I guess we kind of are one. And that makes me think about how everyone else's family is different and special in its own way. And when I introduce

Ellie to people, I don't say she's my half a sister. I just say she's my sister. My big sister. Just creative, funny, infuriating, beautiful, passionate, sometimes moody, always fabulous Ellie.

And I can't imagine my life without her.

For more fantastic reads log on to
www.fiction.usborne.com

For loads of fun stuff, fab downloads
and top secret info check out
www.kellymckain.co.uk

Also by Kelly McKain
TOTALLY LUCY

Makeover Magic
Lucy tries her makeover magic on the shy new girl at school.
ISBN: 9780746066898

Fantasy Fashion

Can Lucy design a fab enough outfit to win a fashion comp?
ISBN: 9780746066904

Boy Band Blues
Lucy's thrilled to be asked to style a boy band for a school comp.
ISBN: 9780746066911

Star Struck
Lucy's in an actual film! Can she get her cool designs noticed?
ISBN: 9780746070611

Picture Perfect
Will crossed wires ruin Lucy's plans for a surprise birthday party?
ISBN: 9780746070628

Style School
Lucy's started a secret Style School club, but will Mr. Cain find out?
ISBN: 9780746070635

Summer Stars
The girls enter a beach party dance comp together on their hols!
ISBN: 9780746080177

Catwalk Crazy
Can Lucy uncover the secret saboteur of her charity fashion show?
ISBN: 9780746080184

Planet Fashion
Will Lucy's planet-friendly makeover on Tilda's bedroom get on TV?
ISBN: 9780746080191

Best Friends Forever
It's the girls' ultra-glam prom...but who will Lucy go with?
ISBN: 9780746080207